Kansas Fury

Cal Ventner knew he was being pushed off the range, that the band of killers who had moved into the small township of Mason Bend had no fear of the law there and that Sheriff Colman was probably in cahoots with them. His cattle were being rustled until his herd had dwindled to less than half of what it had been, and daily his men were being ambushed and killed on the range.

He knew that there was only one answer to the problem that faced him: he needed a handful of men who were handy with their guns, men who feared nothing and who could help him clean up the territory. Something which the law seemed unable to do. But such men were hard to find. . . .

Then one man rode into the ranch and asked for a job, saying he would do anything. Ventner noticed right away the guns the man wore, tied down and with their handles rubbed smooth through constant use. So he hired this man on the spot, figuring that one man would be better than none in this battle with the killers. But would it be enough?

Kansas Fury

CARL EDDINGS

A Black Horse Western

ROBERT HALE · LONDON

© 1964, 2004 John Glasby
First hardcover edition 2004
Originally published in paperback as
Kansas Fury by Chuck Adams

ISBN 0 7090 7603 7

Robert Hale Limited
Clerkenwell House
Clerkenwell Green
London EC1R 0HT

Typeset by
Derek Doyle & Associates, Liverpool.
Printed and bound in Great Britain by
Antony Rowe Limited, Wiltshire

CHAPTER 1

THE COMING OF THE KILLERS

They rode into the tension-filled township of Mason Bend one evening shortly before sundown, and more than two dozen people in the streets saw them ride their horses up to the sheriff's office and rein in in front of it before slipping from their saddles and making their way inside. There were five of them in the band, and with the Colts tied down in their holsters, they also carried Winchesters in the slings across the saddles. The small sounds of conversation soon died and the townsfolk of Mason Bend were unaware, at that moment, that they had witnessed the beginning of a savage era of lawlessness which had come to the territory.

Inside the office, Sheriff Colman wiped the sweat from the lined flesh of his forehead with the back of his sleeve.

'I heard you boys were riding into town some time,' he said, swallowing a trifle nervously. His eyes shone in a face that looked like a well-aged skull. 'You figgering on staying long?'

'We might be,' said the man who stood directly opposite him. 'Long enough to make sure we run Ventner off the range.'

Colman's thin brows lifted a little. 'Ventner? He ain't an easy man to scare, Carson.'

The big man grinned and he kept on grinning at the sheriff. 'Now that's jest too bad, Colman, because me and my brothers aim to scare him real good. Brad here and Matt have waited a long time to settle things with Ventner; and Jeb Silver and Clem Hagberg are with us on this deal.'

The smile on Bart Carson's face faded swiftly. He stared at the sheriff, his eyes hard like chips of agate, his mouth a straight line. His right hand hovered suggestively above the butt of the Colt.

'You with us on this deal, Colman?' he grated, an odd edge to his voice. 'They told us in Dodge that you were a man we could make a deal with. Reckon you ain't exactly glad to have Ventner here. Pretty big man they say, with plenty of cattle in that herd of his. Good ranch, too, and a handful of men who help him run the place.'

'You figgerin' on taking over that ranch, maybe?'

Colman got to his feet and moved around the side of the desk. The star on his shirt glinted brilliantly in the last red rays of the setting sun.

'We aim to do just that,' said Matt Carson harshly. 'We've thought it over for five years; five years spent in the jailhouse in Dodge. And all that time in there we kept getting the same answer. Cal Ventner testified against us and it was his testimony at the trial that got us the prison sentence. We aim to collect payment for that – in full.' There was no mistaking the meaning behind the other's words. 'Now are you with us, Sheriff. We don't need you, but it would make things easier for us if we knew exactly where we stood. They tell us that you're the law in Mason Bend. We aim to have the law on our side when it comes to a showdown with Ventner.'

Colman made up his mind fast. He had heard of these five men long before they had ridden into Mason Bend;

knew their reputation. Each had killed more than a score of men, whether in fair fight or not, no one knew. Outlaws, crooks, gamblers, rustlers – they were all of these, and more besides.

'I don't know what your fight is with Ventner,' he said slowly, wiping his forehead again, 'but you'll find it. He won't scare easy, and he didn't build up that herd by being afraid.'

Bart Carson grinned again. He sat down, straddling a chair backwards and placing his arms along the back, not once taking his eyes off the sheriff.

'I don't care how he feels about it, that won't make any difference. We'll be staying in Mason Bend for some time. Seems a nice little place; I reckon we'll soon get to like it here.'

There was a long, dead silence in the office. Sheriff Colman, short and stocky, running to fat, licked his lips and glanced up at Carson and his four companions. He ran his hand over his chin, but his fingers moved stiffly.

Bart sat quite still for several moments, then got to his feet, moving with a lithe agility that belied his bulk.

'Where's the best hotel in this town, Sheriff?' he asked.

'There's only the one. Over on the other side of the street thirty yards along. The best grub in town is there.'

'Reckon that's where we'll stay, then.'

The gunslingers filed out of the sheriff's office, out into the dusty street. There were still small knots of people on the boardwalks, men lounging in wooden, tilt-back chairs, seeking the cool of the evening after the heat of the day, men who watched the three brothers and their two companions pull themselves up into the saddle and ride along the darkening street to the hotel.

Inside the office, Sheriff Colman took off his hat and dropped it carelessly on to his desk. Then he lit the lamp, slid the glass cover over it, and sat down tiredly in his chair. He sat there for a long time, staring straight ahead of him, listening to the sounds in the street outside, a weary man trapped by his own conscience and his forgotten obligations.

When he had first been sworn in as sheriff of Mason Bend three years before, when old Matt Carlew had been shot down in the street in front of the hotel by a bunch of outlaws, he had made up his mind that he wouldn't end up that way. Since then he had learned a lot of things, things that a man learns only when he is afraid and when he knows that to keep a whole skin he has thrown in his lot with men outside of the law, that instead of upholding the law in the territory, he was condoning the killings and the rustlings which had taken place around Mason Bend since his stay in office.

Yes, Sheriff Colman wore a star on his shirt, could call out a posse of men to hunt down any man, could shoot a man in the back and claim that he had done it to prevent that man from running away from the law. But he could never escape his own conscience, could not forget the fact that he was a coward, that he had to continue this way now, that he had committed himself to working with the outlaws and hellions.

He did his best to tell himself that there had been nothing else he could have done, that if he hadn't fallen in with the plans of these men he would have been shot, and someone else would have replaced him as sheriff, and that there was no doubt the man chosen would have been in the pay of these gunslingers, might even have been one of them, and things in Mason Bend would have been worse than they were now.

But the thought brought him no comfort. He got to his feet and walked over to the window, looking along the almost deserted street. He could see the horses tethered in front of the hotel. Evidently the men had not yet taken the mounts along to the livery stables.

They're like buzzards circling the sunshot sky, he thought wearily, resting his hands on the wooden ledge, *they can smell death and slaughter, know where the carcasses are, where the killings will start, and they come moving in from Abilene and Dodge, their guns low, butts smooth from constant use, looking only for an excuse to kill.*

He stood there for a long moment. There was the sound of a tinkling piano from the nearby saloon, and a few moments later he saw three of the strangers, the Carson brothers, come out of the hotel, walk their mounts to the livery stable, and then return along the street, pushing open the batwing doors of the saloon and going inside. There was no sign of the other two gunslingers who had been with them.

Damn it, he thought tightly. *If they meant to make trouble for Cal Ventner, there was nothing he could do about it. It would be suicide to try to stop them.*

He knew their reputation, knew them for ruthless killers, men wanted in half a dozen states. In the drawer of his desk there were a dozen posters offering rewards for their capture dead or alive. He wondered how they had managed to get out of the jail in Dodge. Not that it mattered much now – they were here in Mason Bend, and he couldn't see any U.S. Marshal riding into town to hunt down these five men.

Cal Ventner made a slow swing around the perimeter wire at the north end of the ranch. The ranch house itself was the best part of two miles away to the east. He came to the end of the meadow and ran on between tall, black hedges of pine. Here, just beyond the rich, green grass, the country was rough, with huge tumbled boulders that marked the beginning of the rocky land which stretched away to the north in an almost unbroken line before it dwindled away in the Badlands, the desert country that ran on clear to the border more than fifty miles away.

Twilight came on, would linger briefly, until it gave way

to night. As he rode, sitting tall and straight in the saddle, a grey-haired man in his late forties, he kept a watchful eye on the country around him, taking in the long fence where it marked his property from the barren ground, acutely aware of the nagging worry in his mind. Now and then he pulled his mount to a walk to give it a breathing spell, but he hated the delay, and could scarcely abide it, conscious of the fact that someone was trying to run him off the range, that he might, even here, discover signs of this.

Less than three hours after the Carson brothers had ridden into town he had known of it, had guessed at the reason for them being there, but he had not figured that they would try to destroy him like this. During the past three weeks he had lost more than three hundred head of cattle, rustled on the plain, driven off the range to some place known only to those men.

Worse still, he had lost two men, shot down from ambush before they had had a chance to defend themselves, and it was this thought which dominated him now, and he cursed himself for ever having permitted those men to be sent to prison back in Dodge, when he had had the chance of letting the mob string them up from the nearest tree outside of the town.

He had not figured that they would have found him as soon as this, nor that they would have dared to set themselves up quite openly in Mason Bend, clearly operating against the law. His lips tightened into a grim, hard line. He knew where he stood with these gunhawks now, knew that he would get no help from the sheriff to run them down and drive them out of the territory. Colman was definitely in with them, but that was to be expected. Colman was a coward. He would never dare to stand up to professional killers such as these.

Reaching a flat stretch, he gave his mount its head, set the horse forward at a steady canter. The night air blew cool against his face and the twilight faded abruptly, night sweeping in from the east, the stars shining out in their thousands through the black sky. Here he was high up, with the hills rising steeply on his left, and the whole weight of them seemed to press down on him, to be crushing forward as if ready to topple down in a sliding of rock and granite.

Creeks ran down the steep slopes, watered by the spring rains high in the hills, and these provided the moisture so necessary to the life on the spread. Without that water, the grass would wither and die, and there would be no sustenance for the cattle he bred there. In the past this had been his only real problem. Now, something more immediate had come up to take its place.

Reaching the bend in the trail where it forked back in the direction of the ranch, he drifted forward with caution. He had topped a low rise when he came in sight of the horses, tethered fifty yards away, their outlines just visible in the dark. Reining swiftly, he sat taut and still in the saddle, trying to identify those mounts. He felt reasonably certain that they were none of his, and he studied his situation, looking about him closely for any sign of the men.

Carefully he slid from the saddle, pulled his rifle from its boot and crouched down, moving forward a couple of feet. There were three horses there, he felt sure, with possibly another further among the trees. But where were the men? He searched with eyes and ears for the slightest movement, the faintest sound which would tell him where they were, and what they were doing on his land.

Then, quite suddenly and without warning, the sound of a revolver shot bucketed through the clinging stillness. Swiftly he lifted his head, flinching involuntarily, although some hidden instinct told him that the shot had not been intended for him. The horses in the distance flung up their heads at the sudden sound.

The party came out into the open two minutes later. Five men bunched closely together, two of them carrying rifles. Even though it was dark and they were too far away to make identification certain, he felt positive that these were the Carson brothers and those two men they had brought with them.

He veered in to the side of the hill, his back scraping the rocks as he settled himself, resting the rifle on one of the boulders in front of him, sighting along it as he steadied the weapon.

The party drifted forward, moving towards the horses. They did not have the slightest idea that he was there, were not looking for trouble from any quarter.

He waited, took up the trigger's slack as he watched the leading man move into his sights. Once he had the other's shoulders in the notch of the sight, he squeezed the trigger, felt the rifle kick against his shoulder. He knew that he had missed even though the man fell back, stumbling against the man just behind him.

Lead spattered around him as the outlaws opened up, crouching down low near their horses. At first their fire was well wide of the mark. None of them had seen from which direction his shot had come, and they were firing blindly into the night. Swiftly he fired again, snapping more shots into the trees where the gunhawks were hidden. The sharp, cracking echoes crashed back at him from the hills. Every muscle in him was so tight that he began to ache, and his legs were twisted with cramp as he tried to shift his body into a fresh position.

The firing from the trees ceased for a moment. He sat back, figuring that the other were possibly reloading, then saw that this was not the case, that they were rushing for their mounts, swinging themselves up into the saddle, pulling hard on the reins, wheeling the horses away from the trees out into the open, away from where he lay.

He fired a couple of shots after them as they rode off,

still bunched together, but it was almost impossible for him to make out any target now, and he pushed himself slowly to his feet, the rifle in his right hand, and the sound of hoofbeats fading into the distance, echoing in his ears.

Evidently the gunslingers had not wanted to tie in with someone they could not see, and were unsure of how many men were there, crouched down in a well-shielded position. They were taking no chances, had obviously done what they had set out to do, and were content to pull out as quickly as possible before any of them were hit.

Gaining the shelter of the pines, he stopped. then whistled up his mount, peering into the darkness that lay all about him now. He fought his way over rough ground, leading the horse, and when he discovered nothing there to account for the shot he had heard, he mounted up and rode down into the valley.

Fifty yards further on he found what he was seeking. He dismounted slowly and knelt beside the man who lay near the small creek, turned him over gently and stared down into the grey-blurred face. Ned Steeler, the man he had sent to check along the perimeter fence. Already the other's face was cold, and as he felt his body he came across the wet stickiness on his shirt, bent closer and saw the blood that stained the cloth between the man's shoulder blades.

A sudden sense of fury seized him. So that was what had happened. The third man to die. Shot in the back like the other two without warning, the shot fired from ambush.

There was no sign of the other's horse, and he guessed the animal had fled, would find its way back to the corral. Bending again, he hooked his hands under Steeler's arms and pulled him up, heaving him across the front of his own saddle, then climbed up behind him, urging the horse forward in the direction of the ranch.

There were lights showing through the windows of the ranch as he rode into the courtyard, reined the horse in in

13

front of the porch. The door opened a minute later and the figure of a girl stood outlined against the yellow light. She stepped forward, staring up at him, still unable to make him out in the darkness.

'That you, Father?' she called in a clear voice.

'Just go back inside, Virginia,' he answered tightly. 'I'll be there in a little while. Something I got to do first.'

For a moment she stood stock still, then she came forward a little way, head tilted back.

'Something has happened again.' Her voice held a tight note now. 'Who was it this time?'

He knew there was no chance of lying to her, that she had already seen the body lying across the saddle.

'Ned Steeler,' he said in a harsh voice. 'They shot him in the back out in the North Meadow. I might have saved him if I'd got there a minute sooner. I spotted their horses among the trees, then heard the shot. I fired at them but they mounted up and rode off.'

'Did you see who they were?'

Strangely, there was no fear in her voice, as he had expected. Her tone was emotionless, empty, as if she had been anticipating this, and been waiting for him to ride back with the news.

'I didn't need to see who they were,' he gritted. 'I know. The same five men who've been rustling my cattle and shooting down the rest of my men. The Carson brothers and those two gunslingers they brought with them.'

'You've met these men somewhere before, Father?'

She stepped back as he swung out of the saddle. A couple of hands came round the corner of the ranch, moved towards them, and he handed the horse over to them, telling them to take the body down and arrange for the sheriff to be notified. Then he followed his daughter into the house.

Virginia was standing in the corner of the room, waiting for him, as he closed the door softly behind him. There was a stony look on her face as she glanced towards him. Slowly he sank down on to the low couch, stretched his legs out in front of him.

Then he nodded his head very slowly, almost imperceptibly. 'Yes, I've met them all before. It was some years ago now, back East. There'd been a lot of stage robberies and a train had been held up by five masked bandits. Wells Fargo were hunting them down, but I managed to get a good look at a couple of them when they held up their last stage. I gave evidence against them when they were arrested and charged in Dodge. The circuit judge sentenced them to fifteen years in prison. Somehow they must have got out of jail, and now they've managed to trail me here – it wasn't a difficult thing to do, I reckon.'

The colour had gone entirely from the girl's face now, and she took a hesitant step forward, putting out one hand to touch her father's shoulder.

'But they won't stop at rustling the herd, or shooting down the hands. It's you they want, and when they've had their play with you, they'll kill you. Why don't you ride into town and warn Sheriff Colman?'

'Colman!' He almost spat the word out as if it left a nasty taste in his mouth. 'I told him when Sweeney was killed in the South Meadow. He just said he'd look into it, that was all.'

Ventner got to his feet and began to pace the room. 'I reckon he must be in with these killers. He's scared, and if he figures there might be something in it for him, he'll throw in his lot with them and that'll be the end of it as far as the law in Mason Bend is concerned.'

'But what can we do?'

'Try to fight them, I suppose. I doubt if they've talked anyone else in town to help them, apart from the sheriff, and he'll just see to it that these killers get a free hand, can do what they like.' Every word was a curse as he spoke.

He sat down again, body slumped forward a little. It

wasn't unexpected, this double-crossing by the sheriff. Ever since Colman had been elected to the post he had shown himself utterly unable to maintain law and order in the town and surrounding territory.

Perhaps he ought to try to fight. Perhaps it was the only way left open to him now. These men wouldn't stop until they had destroyed him utterly, and although he was not really afraid for himself, he was afraid of what they might do to Virginia.

All of this that he had built up here, this cattle empire in the heart of Kansas, had been for her alone. One day it would all belong to her, and he wanted to make certain that when that day came there would be no more killers, no more outlaws, to fight. There would be peace in this part of the territory. But his thoughts were sudden and harsh to his mind, and the huge, gnarled hands tightened into hard-balled fists in front of him.

'We can't run,' he said, his voice almost a whisper. 'We have to fight, it's the only thing we can do. But we don't have the men to fight these gunhawks. We don't have the kind of man we need. To fight these men you have to have a man used to killing, a man like them but on the right side of the law – and such men are hard to find.'

A minister came down from one of the small settlements in the hills, came out to the ranch, conducted the funeral service for Steeler, said a handful of words over the grave by the side of the corral, and then went on his way again after he had eaten his dinner.

An hour later Cal Ventner hitched up the team and rode into Mason Bend to see Sheriff Colman. The town was quiet as he rode in. An hour past high noon, the street was hot and dusty, a river of shimmering brown through the middle of the town. On either side the saloons and stores were silent, and the few men who lounged on the boardwalks eyed him curiously, but without a second glance as he drove the gig past them and drew rein in front of the sheriff's office.

Out of the corner of his eye he noticed the five horses tethered in front of the hotel, guessed that they belonged to the men who had sworn to destroy him, and in spite of himself felt a little quiver of apprehension pass through his stomach as he climbed down and went into the sheriff's office. Colman glanced up at him from his seat behind the desks, gave him a curt nod by way of greeting, and motioned him ungraciously to the chair in front of the desk.

'What brings you into town this early, Cal?' he asked warily. There was a curious expression at the back of the watery blue eyes.

'I came to tell you that another of my men was shot last night, cut down from ambush at the north end of the spread.'

The other's face showed no surprise.

'I did hear something about that,' he agreed.

'You going to do anything about it, Sheriff?'

'Now see here, Cal. I'll admit that this is the third killing on your spread in a few days, but my hands are tied unless you can give me any concrete evidence as to the identity of the killers.'

'We got no argument along those lines,' said Ventner grimly. 'But this time I've got the evidence. I was there when the shooting happened. I saw the five men just after they shot Steeler. *I know who they were.*'

For the first time the look of almost bored equanimity on the sheriff's feature vanished. He sat forward in his chair, arms resting on the desk, eyeing Ventner sharply. 'You *sure* you saw 'em right, Cal? If'n you're going to start accusing somebody of killing your men, you'd better be sure of your facts. It won't be easy for me to arrest anybody just on your say-so.'

'I figured that!'

There was a deliberate insult in the rancher's tone as he stared at the other, saw the sheriff's gaze slide away guiltily.

'I recognised the Carson brothers and those two gunhawks they brought with them into Kansas, out from Dodge. I know plenty about all five of 'em, and I know why they're trying to ruin me.'

'When did this shooting happen?' asked the other, thoughtfully.

'Less than an hour after sundown.'

'But it would be dark then. How can you be sure you recognised them?'

Ventner smiled thinly. 'I saw them clearly, Sheriff. Now are you going to arrest those five killers for murder – or ain't you?'

Colman remained silent for several moments. Only the knuckles standing out white on the backs of his hands showed the strain he was under, knowing that the man in front of him was watching every reaction closely.

Then he shook his head wearily, got to his feet and stood looking down at the rancher.

'I'd like to help you, Cal. I've known you for a long time, even before I was elected sheriff of this town, and I know you're a good and sincere man, but even such men can be mistaken. I know what's driving you as far as these five men are concerned. But so far they've been in town for some time now, and I've got no proof that they've stepped outside of the law for one single minute. I can't go across to the hotel and arrest them on a charge of murder just because you figure you saw them after Steeler had been shot.'

'You mean that you daren't do it,' blazed Ventner. He pushed back his chair so violently that it fell over with a clatter, but he did not turn to pick it up. Instead, he glared at the sheriff, and for a moment his hands hovered close to the butts of the Colts at his waist. Then he controlled himself with an effort. Shooting down this man would do no good; not at the present time, anyway. It would only result in himself being tried for murder, and he would not be of any help to Virginia in jail, waiting to be tried for murder.

Colman smiled thinly, noticing the way the other's hands dropped from the guns.

'That's better, Ventner. I don't want to have to arrest you, but I'll have to do it if you try anything as far as these men are concerned. I can understand your feelings towards them. Your evidence put them in jail and you figure that they've come here to have their revenge on you.' He shrugged.

'Best ride back to the ranch and forget it, Cal.'

There was a note almost of pleading in his voice now, as if he realised that the other would not heed this advice, and he himself could foresee the trouble which was going to arise.

'All right, Sheriff – it seems you ain't going to do anything to help me. Maybe you're in this with these killers, maybe not. I don't know. But I'll tell you this. I'm giving my men orders to shoot any strangers coming on to my spread from now on.'

'If these men are the professional killers you seem to think they are, you might find it difficult to get hands once you set yourself up against them. There aren't many hands to be had who'll agree to be gunslingers as well.' He measured the other with an appraising glance. 'I don't want to give advice, that isn't my job. But if I were you I'd get out of this territory while you still have the chance. That's a friendly warning, Cal.'

For a long moment Ventner stared at the other in silence, then he spun on his heel and stalked out through the doorway into the street. A swift glance to his left and he saw that the five horses which had been tethered to the hitching rail in front of the hotel when he had entered the sheriff's office were no longer there. There was a little tremor of uneasiness in his mind as he climbed back on to the buckboard and drove out of town, heading back along the trail in the direction of the ranch.

Cal Ventner rode slowly, a man who was dead tired, but filled with a weariness which had nothing to do with lack of sleep. There was a growing fear deep within him, something which he could not throw off no matter how hard he tried. Had those five killers ridden into Mason Bend only a few weeks before? It seemed to him like a century.

He himself had come to this part of Kansas more than twenty years before, when this territory had been part of a vast wilderness, totally unfit for grazing cattle, where nothing grew but the thorn bushes and the mesquite. But the moment he had seen the place he had been filled with a dream.

Slowly, over the years which had passed since that day, he had witnessed his dream becoming reality. It had not been easy work, building up the ranch, the barns and the stockade which had eventually become the corral. But this had been the place where he had decided to put his roots, where he had brought Anne, Virginia's mother, and they had been happy in those days, even though the times had been hard.

He had marked out the boundaries of the spread which he had claimed. He had ridden it day after day, mapping the place in his mind, seeing how it would look in ten, twenty years time. It had been a lot of ground, and there had been times, he had been forced to admit himself, when it had seemed impossible that they would ever succeed.

But by good fortune and hard work, they had overcome each obstacle as it had presented itself, they had started the herd with a handful of cows and bulls, and bred them over the years until they had numbered several thousand, and there had been plenty of grass on which they had been able to feed.

In those days they had said he was a fool to grow beef there, that it would be a long way to the market, a long and dangerous trail before they reached the railhead. But he had known with a deep and lasting conviction that the men of the country would not have been able to build their huge cities without beef, that they needed it desperately to feed their growing millions, and that there would always be a market for cattle.

There had been men who called themselves his friends and others who were his enemies and, in the end, they had both become the same, so that he had been unable to trust either. Where he had flourished and prospered, others had been forced to sell out and go back east, or they had taken the gamble and headed west when the yellow gold had been discovered in California. Whatever the cause, he was now the largest rancher in that part of the territory, and he still had his enemies.

He felt his lips tighten hard in his face. There were five of them now, roaming the territory somewhere, possibly watching him even at that moment from up in the hills that bordered the trail at this point. And these men were perhaps the most dangerous enemies he had ever had.

Sitting tall and straight on the buckboard, he let his eyes wander warily over the tall rocks on either side of the trail, especially where they crushed down close to it on either side, rising for a sheer fifty feet or more, red sandstone that shone brilliantly in the heat of the late afternoon sun. Even though he was cautious, ready for trouble, when it did come he was almost too late to save himself.

He turned a sharply angled bend in the trail, flickered his gaze above him as he spurred the horses forward. A rock bounced down the sheer side of the canyon wall, then another. Only small rocks falling swiftly in a shower of tiny pebbles and dust, but enough to give the warning to the experienced eyes and ears of the man on the buckboard.

There was sudden movement high above him, a gathering of rocks as they began to slide, rolling and rushing towards him from the very top of the canyon wall. There was no time to pause and think of what was best to be done. Time only for the instinctive motion which saved his life. No sense in stopping the horses, in trying to pull them back. The landslide would be upon him before he could do that.

Instead, he slashed at them savagely with the whip, felt the wagon lurch and sway as it bounded forward, swinging dangerously from side to side of the trail. A rough, outjutting crop of red rock scraped along his arm as he swung dangerously close to the canyon wall. Something came hurtling down out of the air and struck him with a sickening force on the side of the temple, throwing him to one side. He had instinctively thrown up one arm in an effort to shield himself from the rock, but he had been far too late. For a moment he almost lost consciousness, holding grimly on to the reins as the horses threatened to jerk them out of his slackening grip.

Then there was the full, savage thunder of the landslide crashing down just behind him, blotting out the trail at that point, obliterating it completely.

He thought he heard dim yells from somewhere above him, followed by the sharp barks of rifles, but he could not be sure, and now that the horses had the bit between their teeth there was no stopping them.

Fighting to hold on to his buckling consciousness, he gripped the reins tightly in both hands, slitting his eyes against the glare of sunlight, aware that there was the warm stickiness of blood on his forehead just above his right eye, running down his face.

Those sudden cries from the top of the canyon had told him that it had been no accident, those rocks rushing down like that just at the moment when he happened to be passing underneath. Someone had deliberately started that slide, and he could guess who it was. But as Sheriff Colman had taken such pains to point out to him, he had no definite proof of his suspicions.

The canyon opened out a moment later and he was in

more open country. He knew that now he would be able to see the men if they tried to follow him, guessed that he would possibly be able to outrun them, knowing that they would have to saddle up and then lead their mounts down the tortuous, twisting path from the top of the rocks.

A quarter of a mile further on he pulled the horses to a more reasonable trot, his ears attuned to any sound behind him. Within half an hour he knew that he was not being pursued.

The Carson brothers would have given up the idea of trying to kill him now. But he knew they would not have given up altogether. The showdown would come soon, and there was little he could do to prevent or even delay it.

But what to do now? He knew that Colman had spoken the truth when he had claimed that very few, if any, of his hands would fight these killers if it came to a showdown. He had hired them to herd cattle for him, not to stand up to men like the Carsons.

He dabbed at the wound on the side of his head, noticed that the bleeding had stopped now, wincing whenever his fingers touched it.

The spread burst upon him twenty minutes later as he rode through the gap in the perimeter wire. His breath was torturing his lungs as he rode into the courtyard in front of the house and climbed unsteadily from the wagon. Virginia must have been watching for him, concerned, for she came out almost instantly, ran across to him, placing her arm around his shoulder.

'Father!' she said. 'Thank God you're still alive. Are you all right?'

The violent nerve strain of that ride back from town throbbed incessantly at the back of his eyes as he stumbled up on to the porch.

She gave a quick little gasp as he half-turned his head. 'You're hurt?'

'Nothin' much,' he said harshly. 'Just hit by a piece of

falling rock, that's about all.'

'Better go inside and sit down. I'll bathe it for you. It looks a nasty bruise.'

She did not question him further until he was drinking a cup of hot coffee, seated on the low couch, a bandage around his head. Looking up, he saw the shadow cross her eyes as she seated herself in the chair opposite him.

'You didn't get any help from Sheriff Colman,' she began. It was more of a statement than a question, and he knew that she was not expecting him to answer it, but he shook his head.

'I thought not. You must be right. He's either in with them or he's scared of what they might do to him if he doesn't do as they say.'

Her voice was like visible pain, the angry cry of tortured emotions, burned raw. She had no control over what she said now, knew only that it had to be said, one way or another.

'If they think they can drive us out of this ranch, after all the work you've done in building it up into what it is now, then they're mistaken. We'll fight them.'

'You want 'em to come here looking for us?' he demanded. 'You want to get yourself killed? They won't just kill me now, you know, they'll destroy you, destroy everything I've made.'

'We can fight.'

'What with?' He shook his head wearily. 'I've lived with dreams too long. This isn't a dream. This is the reality. We can't fight these men. We haven't got the right to ask any of the hands to stand against such killers.'

'Then we'll have to find ourselves some men who can stand up to them,' she declared passionately. 'If that's the only solution.'

'Such men aren't easy to find. You won't find them in Mason Bend, otherwise those five gunhawks would have been run out of town long ago.'

He thought briefly of Sheriff Colman in his office, standing up to him, trying to meet his gaze, blustering all the time; a frightened man making a faint cry for manhood, knowing that he had failed miserably. The thought brought him no sense of consolation. The sheriff didn't have to take any real chances, he thought bitterly. He could sit in that office of his, safe and secure, with the knowledge that so long as he did not go against the Carsons he would be quite safe.

And if he did manage to kill one of that gang when they came the next time, the others would either shoot it out with him, or they would even ride on back into town, get a posse and come out after him, could even bring the sheriff with them to make it all legal.

His head jerked around at a sudden commotion at the door. At the same time there was the sound of hoofbeats in the courtyard outside, the sound of a horse being reined to a halt. He got to his feet as one of the hands came in.

'Somebody just rode in, Boss,' he called loudly. 'Looks like he wants a job.'

Ventner walked slowly to the door, went out on to the porch and looked up into the red sunlight against which the man on horseback was silhouetted.

His first impression was of a tall, slender man dressed in black, sitting easily in the saddle, and with a deadly calm about him that was striking and instantly apparent. A slow and climbing tenseness seemed to be focused on the man.

Then Ventner's gaze dropped to the guns the man wore, tied down low, with the handles rubbed smooth. His gaze flicked back to the clear grey eyes that watched him unblinkingly from beneath the dark brows, and he knew instinctively that there was something about this man, something dangerous. . . .

CHAPTER 2

THE DANGEROUS ONE

The hand that rested on the pommel of the saddle was steady; stone steady. No use to ask what kind of a man this was, although for an instant the thought lived in Ventner's mind as he stood there in the courtyard, watching the man who sat easily in the saddle.

'Were you looking for something, stranger?' he asked quietly.

The other shrugged.

'Thought you might be needing a hand on the ranch,' he said softly.

'Riding or fighting?'

'Anything you care to name.' The tall man narrowed his eyes slightly, studying Ventner closely. 'I ain't particular.' He paused. 'Your name Ventner?'

'That's right – how did you know?'

'There's talk in Mason Bend. They say you've been losing cattle – and men. Somebody must sure want you out of the territory, and they ain't caring how they do it.'

Ventner screwed up his lips. 'Just who are you?' He relaxed a little as though he had just been under a great strain.

'Mark Farrell, up from Dodge.' A pause, then: 'You still looking for a hand?'

'Could be.' Ventner nodded slowly, knew that his first impression of this man had been right. Most of Kansas knew that name, knew the reputation of the man who sat looking down at him, knew of the danger that rode with him, the sudden death that was never very far behind. There were those who said there were wanted posters out for him as far south as the Mexican border. There were others who were ready to testify to the quickness of his guns, to the death that lived in his eyes, in the deceptive little movement he made as he half-bowed by way of introduction.

All of this, Ventner knew, and for the first time, since the Carson brothers had ridden into Mason Bend, there was a faint stirring of hope within him. He gave the other one last, appraising glance, then nodded.

'Wages fifteen dollars a month. That all right?' he said abruptly. 'There may be trouble. You've heard something in Mason Bend. All of that was true and more beside.'

Farrell swung swiftly from the saddle.

'Suits me. I take it I'm hired.'

'That's right.' Ventner turned, moved towards the house. 'Better put up your mount and then come inside. You can bunk with the rest of the boys, but I'd like to talk to you first.'

Farrell watched him go for a moment, then followed one of the hands towards the stables. That was how he came to the Ventner ranch. There had been no hand-clasp, no ceremony. Just the brief nod from Ventner and the curt order to talk things over with him as soon as his mount had been stabled.

The afternoon was more than half gone and the heat head of the day had reached its height as Mark Farrell made his way across the dusty courtyard, towards the ranch. Nothing relieved the heat. It hung over everything with a hot, heady pressure like the slap of a mighty hand, making every breath an individual labour.

There was a pot of hot, black coffee on the table in the room, and Virginia Ventner brought in a cup, poured coffee into it, and nodded towards the tin of condensed milk and sugar box. She continued to watch him as he sat down in the chair facing her father; she seemed puzzled and uncertain at what she saw, and the expression hardened her face a little. He knew that she was trying to guess what kind of a man he really was, and if there was any truth in the rumours that must have reached this part of the territory.

In a man he might have been angry at that kind of look, but somehow her gaze did not trouble him, and he switched his eyes to Cal Ventner, eyeing him closely from beneath lowered black brows.

There was a kind of challenge in the older man's eyes as he locked his gaze with Farrell's. The heavy head was drawn down a little on the other's neck, lower lip thrust forward.

Then Ventner said harshly: 'I reckon you know why I hired you back there, just like that without asking too many questions.'

Farrell nodded.

'It seemed to me that you wanted a man who could use a gun, that you have enough men here to handle the cattle, if you're left in peace to run things.'

'That's right. Maybe you know who's trying to run me out of the territory?'

'There was talk of the Carson brothers being in town.' Farrell spoke easily, almost casually. There was a tiny flicker of something hard and unholy at the back of the grey eyes, but that was the only indication he gave that he might have heard something of these men; that and the slight curling of the fingers in the gloves, as if they were hooked around the handle of a Colt, lining it up on a man's chest.

'They say that you're handy with a gun, that you don't ask too many questions when you have to kill a man.'

'I've managed to stay alive so far.'

'You might find it a little more difficult if you work for me.'

'I might at that,' agreed the other.

He sipped the hot coffee, kept his eyes on the man opposite him, watching him closely, unblinkingly, over the rim of the cup.

'I don't aim to go into details as to why they want to run me off the ranch. That's all water under the bridge now. But there was something in Dodge a few years back when they were arrested and jailed. They ought to have been hung, but they got away with it, and now they're out here, biding their time, looking for revenge. They mean to kill me and take everything I have, and they won't be satisfied until they've done it.'

'I've heard of them.'

Farrell turned his eyes momentarily towards the girl standing near the open door leading into the kitchen. 'They say that three of your men have been shot down from ambush, that the sheriff in town refuses to do anything about it.'

'He's in cahoots with those gunhawks,' Ventner said. 'I rode out there today to ask him for help, told him that another man had been killed last night. He told me I had no proof it was any of those five men who had shot him down, even though I saw them riding away with my own eyes.'

'Could be you're right.' Farrell nodded slowly, draining his cup and setting it on the table in front of him. 'I've heard of these killers. Ain't heard of any sheriff yet who didn't throw in his lot with 'em.'

'I figure you might be able to help me. They tried to kill me on my way back from town, started a rock slide few miles from here. I need a man who's not afraid to stand up to them.'

'You mean that if these men make any more trouble for you, you want them dead?'

The bluntness of his talk brought a faint show of surprise to the other's face, and he heard the girl's sharp intake of breath, but he did not shift his gaze from the other man's face, knowing that his words had arrested Ventner's attention, that the other was watching him with an absorbed, wondering interest.

Finally Ventner swallowed a little, then nodded, shifting his gaze swiftly. 'Yes,' he said, and his voice was little more than a harsh murmur. 'I want them killed.'

Before Mark could speak, Virginia Ventner said throatily: 'You talk as if you've ridden alone too much.'

He tightened his lips a little.

'How do you know that?' he asked.

'Your way of thinking comes from riding alone, and that kind takes you into a lot of strange places, among strange company.'

He nodded indifferently. From the look on her face, he guessed that she was a young woman with her own temper. He saw it come to her face and lips, saw her eyes narrow just a shade and lose warmth.

She said: 'I've heard a lot about you, but how much is true we don't know. Normally, we wouldn't hire a man with your kind of reputation, but—'

'But in the present circumstances you're forced to use drastic means to prevent these outlaws from running you off the range, possibly killing you just to get even with your father.'

'Yes.' Somehow she forced the word out.

He smiled, keeping his penetrating gaze on her, watching with his eyes half-closed. At least, he thought, she was being honest about it. She was still prying him for his worth, he thought, trying to guess at his real character.

Minutes later he went out into the yard. Far off the horizon shimmered in the heat and dust still lay in the air, hazing details, turning the heavens into a harsh yellow glare so that there was little blue in the sky except for a small patch far from the disc of the sun.

He checked his horse, then went over to the bunkhouse, stepped inside. It was cooler there and there was only one man inside, seated at the table, his hands hovering over a well-thumbed deck of cards as he played solitaire idly. He swung to face the door as Mark entered, then got to his feet and gestured with a thumb towards the bunk at the far end.

'That's yours, mister,' he said thinly. He was a small, slender man with rapidly greying hair, old but, Mark guessed, he could still sit straight in the saddle, could still do a real day's work on the ranch whenever it was demanded of him. His watery blue eyes continued to watch Farrell as the other went over to the bunk and dropped his bed roll on it.

'Likely you're wondering,' he said at length, 'why the boss hired you on the spot like that.'

'He already made that quite clear,' Mark told him straightening up. 'He wants the Carson brothers off his neck, and he doesn't want any more of his men killed.'

'So he told you.' The other sat back down at the table, began to lay the cards out once more. He did not look at Farrell as he said: 'I know you by name, Farrell – know that you're a cattleman and a gunfighter.'

'And it's the last that's got you worried.' Mark grinned thinly.

'In a way,' nodded the other. He laid one card on top of another.

'Are you afraid of me?'

A pause – for perhaps the space of three seconds, then the oldster shook his head very slowly. 'No, I'm not afraid of you, Farrell.'

He half-turned in his chair and this time looked straight at the other as he spoke: 'I'm no gunfighter like you. I'm an old man and I've seen killers come and killers go. But I reckon I know a little more about you than most, even though you don't realise it. Sure you've killed men, always in fair fight, and always they've been gunhawks or hired gunslingers, more often than not; they've been wanted by the law, too. I don't figure that you'd shoot down a man like me.'

'Maybe you're right,' said Farrell seriously. 'And you figure that's the reason I rode in here and asked for a job, knowing from what I'd heard in town that the odds were I'd get this one.'

'I don't aim to guess at your reasons, they're your concern. I reckon that every man has to have a code he lives by – and I guess you have yours.'

Farrell went back to his bunk, seated himself on the edge and rolled himself a smoke. When he lighted the cigarette, he leaned back, blew smoke into the air.

Through the smoke he gave the older man a prolonged study. From what he had seen here, there was no one of the right calibre to stand up to men like the Carsons. Their reputation, like his, would have travelled ahead of them and men would be wary about crossing them.

He let his thoughts wander, easing his shoulders back against the head of the bunk. Restlessness continued to bubble up inside his mind and little things out of the past few years formed pictures in his brain, the feelings of the hot sun on his back out there in the desert Badlands, the days of heat when the alkali dust had been thick on his flesh and in his nostrils and lungs, in spite of the bandana around the lower half of his face, when he had ridden bent low over the saddle, trying to shield his eyes from the hurt of the glaring sunlight, long days in the timber country of the mountains, with the sharp smell of the pines in his face and the soft bed of needles underfoot, his mount picking its way carefully down narrow, tortuous trails between huge boulders and outjutting columns of rock.

The faint song of the wind in the mesquite bushes, and long cool nights with a white moon riding high in the heavens, with the stars as faint powderings of light that fell down the slopes of the sky towards the horizon, which was always on the very edge of the world.

There had been the towns where he had been forced to ride through quickly, or skirt them altogether because of the chance of being recognised and brushing with the law, but at the very beginning of it all, the fount from which all of these memories sprang, there was Dodge, a bustling, brawling town on the very frontier, where the trails met, where the cattlemen and the homesteaders fought over the land, and life was cheap.

There had been the long cruel years of the war, and although they had changed him, brought the harsh bitterness into his mind once the South had been defeated, it had been what came after that had brought the change into his life.

The war had taught him how to kill, and it had also taught him that the South had been the defeated side, and there were men from the North who were not going to let them forget it.

The carpetbaggers moved in, in droves, swindled the people, took over the land, made sure they got the rock-bottom prices for their cattle. But worse than these men were the renegade Army men, who had found a new way of continuing with their fighting days and getting rich at the same time. The outlaws who robbed the stages and the trains, killed and plundered, rode wild through the Southern states.

Three of these men had held up the stage a mile outside Dodge on that hot, sultry day all those years before, had held it up and fired blindly into the coach when the passengers had been a little slow in getting out. There had been only two people in the coach that day. The man, a cattleman from Oregon, had merely been shot in the shoulder. The other passenger, Farrell's sister, was killed instantly. He had found her grave three weeks later on the hillside overlooking Dodge, with her name carved on the stone.

He had located the driver of the stage and from him had

been given as accurate a description of the men who had held up that stage as possible; and when they had been brought in three moths later, the Carson brothers, he had known the identities of the men he had to trail and kill.

Before leaving Dodge he had met the doctor who had examined the injured man on the stage. The doctor had said: 'It was such a shame that they had to gun down such a fine and pretty girl like that. She didn't have a gun, they must have done it just for fun.'

It had been that last phrase of the doctor's that had twisted the point of the knife in his mind. Over the years the burden in him had grown until at times it had seemed unbearable. He had tried to find those men, but always the answer had been the same: they were shut up in the jail in Dodge, where they had been locked up after being arrested for another robbery altogether.

Impatiently he had bided his time, knowing that no jail would keep those men for long and that, sooner or later, they would bust out of prison, would become free men again, and his chance to hunt them down like the animals they were, and destroy them, would come.

The burden of his sister's death had had other effects on him, too. It had blistered and destroyed what little faith he had ever had, it had made him hard and tough, disbelieving, had turned him against his fellow creatures until he had become a creature of habit, seeking only revenge, nursing his hatred until the day he would be able to repay his debt to these three killers.

That evening, eating with the rest of the men in the cookhouse, washing down the food with more black coffee, he listened to what had happened on the ranch since the Carson brothers had ridden into Mason Bend, how three men had been killed, shot down from ambush without a chance to defend themselves.

He listened to the quiet, guarded talk of these men, knew that they were brave and honest men, but that they were almost at the limit of their tether. These men were not professional killers. They had signed on to work for Ventner as cattlemen and drovers, not as bodyguards.

That night, as he lay on his bunk with the lights out in the bunkhouse, he turned things over in his mind, reviewing them objectively. He now knew a lot about the situation here on the Ventner spread, knew that things were swiftly heading for the showdown, that it was inevitable, and when it came, either Ventner would back down, or there would be a full-scale range war here, with the men on this spread in the middle of it.

In spite of the fact that he had ridden long and hard during the past few days, cutting across some of the most inhospitable country in the entire state, resting only long enough to give his horse chance to catch its wind, he felt that his mind was still alert and clear.

In Mason Bend he had seen nothing of the men he sought, yet he knew that they were there. There had been talk in the saloon, talk to which he had listened carefully, absorbing everything, and long before he had ridden out of town, heading towards the Ventner spread, he had known that his long search was over, that he had finally caught up with the men he meant to kill; and the knowledge had brought a tight, singing thrill to his mind, a sharpness to his eyes.

Acting by impulse and habit, he lifted his gun from its worn holster and laid it carefully under the straw where it would be close to his hand.

The next morning he ate breakfast in the dining-room of the ranch with Cal Ventner and Virginia. Also at the table was Mort Kennedy, the foreman of the ranch, and a few minutes later Teeler Malloy, the oldster he had first met the previous day, came in and took his place with them.

When he had finished he went out into the yard. At that early hour of the morning, before the full heat of the sun laid a blistering blanket over everything, the air was clear and went down like wine into his lungs. He stared out over the spread towards the high mountains in the distance where they lifted up on the skyline, their peaks tinged red with the rays of the rising sun. It was difficult to judge how far away they were; in that clear air, one tended to under-estimate distance.

There was a herd of prime beef cattle on the slope of a low rise, perhaps two miles distant. Three men were riding them across the slope in the direction of the wide meadow which lay beyond.

'To look at that, you'd never think that there was about to be any trouble, would you, Farrell?'

He turned quickly to see that Ventner had come out of the house and was standing on the porch, rolling a smoke.

'It sure looks mighty peaceful,' he admitted. 'You seem to have a good herd out there. It must be good grazing country here.'

'The best in this neck of the state.' Ventner nodded, licked the paper of his cigarette, thrust it between his lips and lit it, puffing smoke into the still air where it hung like a blue haze in front of his face.

'But that's only part of the herd. There are more than three thousand head on the North Meadow.'

He stepped down on to the white dust of the courtyard. 'That's what I wanted to talk with you about. I didn't want to do it at breakfast, no sense in worrying the others unduly. At the moment, this is only a hunch I've got.'

'Go on,' said Farrell tightly. 'What's on your mind?'

'I've got a feeling that there'll be more of my cattle rustled pretty soon. Since Steeler was killed, things have been quiet on the ranch. They may try tonight or tomorrow night. And they won't hit that herd out there, it'll be the one on the north spread they'll go for. Too far away from the ranch house for me to get any men out there in a hurry.'

Mark's thoughts ran fast and uncertain in his head. The

other stared into the distance, not looking at him. His lips were pressed into a tight line, and there was a worried expression on his features.

'I'd like to get out there myself, be on hand if anything does happen. But I doubt if I'd make it out there, and even if I did, I'd be of little use if they did attack.'

'You want me to ride out there and keep watch on the herd?'

'I'd feel a lot easier in my mind if you did. You want any of the others to saddle up and ride with you?'

Mark pursed his lips. 'How many men have you out there with that part of the herd?'

'Four. They're good men, not the sort to run at the first sign of trouble.'

Mark gave him a keen glance, then shook his head.

'Won't be necessary, then. If the Carsons do come tonight, there'll be enough of us to take care of 'em, unless the sheriff brings a posse with them and throws in his lot openly with these gunhawks.'

He picked his sorrel out of the stable, saddled up, tightening the cinch carefully before swinging up easily into the saddle. No need to check the guns in the well-worn holsters, they were always ready. Since he had come out of the defeated Army of the South, he had made certain that they were ready for anything, and this precaution had on countless occasions saved his life.

Around ten o'clock he left the ranch and headed out to the north, keeping to the broad track for the first part of the way, where it wound up and over the low ridges of grass. The sun was up now, rising swiftly to its zenith, and the dust was hanging in the air over the trail. The heat was a burning pressure on his back and shoulders, heat that rolled back at him from the ridges to the west and east of the trail.

For the first time he realised just how big a spread Cal Ventner had. It must have been the best part of forty miles in the north-south direction, and perhaps half that distance from east to west.

Deliberately he kept the grey eyes half hidden behind the lowered lids, slitting them against the harsh sun glare. Gradually the grassland petered out and gave way to more open, desert country, flinty soil in which very little grew apart from a handful of stunted mesquite bushes and thorn.

Here and there a darting sand lizard showed a brief splash of colour as it skitted away in front of him, startled by the sound of the horse.

He sat easily in the saddle, with a rider's looseness about the build of his body, his hands resting lightly on the pommel in front of him, eyes never still, searching and quartering the horizons, ever watchful, a man who knew from past experience that danger could strike unexpectedly and from the direction one never considered.

Shortly before midday he reached a wide river that ran sluggishly across the trail. Here, at the fording place, the bottom stones of the river bed were scarcely covered by water, and he made camp on the far bank, in the shade of a small clump of trees that grew a little way back from the water.

There was the sharp scent of sage in the air, from leaves burnt brown by the hot desert sun, and he ate jerky beef and made coffee over a small fire, letting the horse drink and then drift a little, knowing that it would not wander far in the burning heat.

Finishing his meal, he stretched himself out in the shade thrown by the trees, tilted his hat over his eyes and the upper half of his face and went to sleep; but even though he slept, he still kept one ear open for trouble.

When he woke, less than an hour later, the shadow of the tree had moved only a little way, and he sat up suddenly, pushing back his hat. Something had woken him and it had not been the touch of the hot sun on his face. There had been something else and he got cautiously to his feet, eyes searching the open ground all about him, taking in everything.

Almost immediately he spotted the haze of dust in the distance, so small that to any other man it might have passed unnoticed. But he saw it and knew what it meant. There was a rider out there and whoever he was, he kept well away from the trail.

He slitted his eyes against the flooding sunlight. He had the unshakeable feeling that the rider had no business to be there, was deliberately riding out in the alkali dust of the desert so that he might not be spotted by anyone keeping a watch on the trail.

He whistled up the sorrel, watered it again, filled his canteen and replaced it on the saddle. Then he swung up, eyed the dust shadow once more, before urging his mount forward.

Here, in the open country, it would be relatively simple for that rider to discover he was being followed. But to the north, before one reached the meadow where the rest of the herd was kept, there was timber country that grew along the eastern slope of the tall hills, dividing the ranch from the desert far to the west, a desert which stretched clear to the border.

Far away he heard the echo of hoofbeats on hard ground, but the sound faded swiftly until only the hot silence lay fast on everything, the hills and trees in the distance shimmering in the heat haze, and only the sound of his own sorrel and its harsh breathing made any sound in the heat of the afternoon.

Up ahead, once that rider reached the pines of the timber country, where the terrain was broken and more rugged, there would be plenty of places where he could shelter, lie in wait for him and pick him off from cover. But he refused to think of this. He knew none of this country and yet he felt no concern on that score. He had been born and bred in country much the same as this, the same pattern of hills and stretches of yellow-white desert, the burning heat, the silence, and the long, cold nights.

By degrees the country roughened. He found it impossible to make as much progress as earlier, and there was now no sign of the man he had been pursuing. The crevices and boulders came down from the heights on his left to meet him, and he rode more slowly and carefully now, eyes swinging from side to side, alert for the slightest movement.

Here the land was deceptive. The trail wound up into the pines, riding high over switchback courses, at intervals coming right on to the bare hillside, with nothing but a steep drop of more than a hundred feet into the canyon floor below.

There was no chance at all of finding that other rider's trail in this country; and at the forefront of his mind he guessed that the other, having spotted him, had hidden among the rocks and boulders and might, at that very moment, be lining up a Winchester on his chest.

The thought gave him a tight feeling in his stomach and he felt the muscles there knot into a hard ball. But he refused to allow it to throw him. He loped the sorrel along the outer edge of the trail as far as possible, keeping well into the open. The sun was sinking swiftly now and very soon he knew it would have dropped behind the hills to the west of him, where they rose up steep and tall, shutting out almost half of the heavens. The north pasture was less than a couple of miles away at the very end of the hilly chain, and he debated whether to turn his mount and head back down into the valley floor, spur the sorrel on to reach the herd before nightfall.

But the mere fact that he had seen this rider spurring his mount as rapidly as possible to the north still troubled him, and his mind persisted in trying to find an explanation for it.

There was always the possibility that someone in the Ventner gang of cowhands was also in cahoots with these killers, passing on valuable information to them, tipping them off when and where the herd would be bedded down at night so that they would know exactly where to go and how many guards to expect.

If that were the case, then there was little doubt that the traitor on the Ventner payroll would ride out as quickly as possible on his heels to warn these outlaws of what had happened. He wasn't sure whether or not his name would mean anything to any of the Carsons. Somehow he doubted it. They would never have bothered to find out the identity of the woman they had killed on that stage, possibly they had not even thought about it after it had happened.

He let the thought run through his mind, felt the tightening of the muscles in his chest, and it was then, when he least expected it, that danger presented itself....

He had been riding between twin rows of tall trees, first year pine, their trunks rising up long and slender against the slowly darkening sky, his gaze on the ground ahead of him because here, if anywhere, was where he was most likely to pick up the trail of the man he felt certain had ridden through less than half an hour before. The trail bent swiftly in front of him, swept around to the right in almost a right angle, and, without warning, there was a slight rustle in the brush less than twenty yards ahead.

Fortunately, he had been holding on lightly to the reins. As he threw himself sideways and down, the vicious crack of the rifle barked in his ears, the loud echoes chasing themselves through the trees until they became dim and muffled by distance. The hum of the slug sounded in his ears, seconds later it struck an exposed outcrop of rock, and went whining off into the distance with the screech of ragged metal.

Hitting the ground hard, he whipped himself round, rolled for the bushes at the edge of the trail. All of the wind had been knocked from his body by the impact of his fall, but he had both Colts in his hands, the weapons whispering from their holsters, almost leaping between his curved fingers of their own accord, his thumbs bringing back the hammers in a single movement.

For an instant he felt a moment's sharp pain in his chest as if he had bruised a rib. Then he sucked air down into his lungs, ignored the stabbing pain, and slithered forward through the brush, making no noise. He had already pinpointed the other's position, less than ten yards inside the undergrowth on the opposite side of the trail.

The man, whoever he was, had been a little too hurried with his shot, a little eager, otherwise he would have waited until he was in his sights before squeezing that trigger. If he had taken his time, it would have been impossible for him to miss at that distance.

He felt more sure of himself now, gently easing his way forward. A moment later he came out on the trail's edge, paused, ears cocked, listening intently for any sound. He guessed that if he had judged this man right, he would be nervous, not the usual kind of bushwhacker. He would be unsure whether that rifle shot had killed or wounded him, and the longer he waited in there, crouched down among the trees and bushes, the more nervous he was going to get and, in a little while, he was going to have to make some kind of move.

Mark crouched there, head well down, content now to bide his time, knowing that he could sit this one out better than the would-be killer. Now that he had a good idea where the man was hiding, he felt certain he was in little danger.

Very softly and without sound, he moved forward on the soft, spongy dirt of the trail, his sorrel standing motionless, as it had been trained to do, a few yards behind him.

He had moved ten yards along the trail when a bullet's vicious explosion battered the clinging silence, cracking against his eardrums as he pulled his head down still further. The breath of the slug's passing touched him and he heard a slap against the spongy bark of a nearby tree.

CHAPTER 3

RUSTLER'S MOON

Seconds passed before he realised that the man had been shooting wild, could not see him, did not know where he was, and had almost hit him only by sheer good luck. He slithered across the narrow track, entered the under-growth on the other side. There was the sharp acrid smell of pine needles in his nostrils.

'Better come out, fella!' Mark spoke loudly and clearly. 'You don't stand a chance. Throw out that Winchester and step out on to the trail with your hands over your head. Pronto!'

No answer. The other was cautious, knew now without a shadow of doubt that the man he had planned to bushwhack was still very much alive and his gamble had not paid off.

Mark could visualise the thoughts that must have been running through the other's mind at that moment. He would be trying to guess his chances of either shooting it out with him, or slipping back into the bushes for his own mount, possibly tied up somewhere close by, and riding out of there alive, knowing that here, in the forest country, it would not be possible to run very fast, that he had waited too long, ought to have kept riding to the north while he had had the chance.

'You've had your chance,' said Mark softly, knowing that the other could hear every word he said. 'Now I'm going to kill you.'

It was a sentence simply said, but every word of it carried the promise of death to the man who lay hidden in the undergrowth.

He heard at last a long sigh come from the man, the exhalation of a man who had been holding his breath tightly bottled in his lungs for fear that it would betray his hiding place, and who could no longer keep it in, the sudden need for air that had betrayed him.

Acting instinctively, Mark moved swiftly to one side, crouched low, the guns ready in his hands. A moment later he knew that he had outguessed the other, that he had reasoned correctly what the man would do. The other had seemed to know that the sudden gusting of air through his open lips had given him away, and he began firing swiftly and with a pure recklessness, bullets cutting and slicing through the bushes around Mark's body.

Somewhere in the near distance he heard a horse begin to thresh around. Some part of his mind, curiously detached from the rest, counted the shots as the man fired, and within seconds he knew that the other had no more in the rifle.

Aiming carefully, he loosed off a couple of shots in the direction of the sound. One of them hit. He heard the sudden sharp intake of breath, the whistle of air going down a constricted throat, muscles corded in sudden agony. Then there was the sound of a heavy body thrusting through the undergrowth, moving away from him. It hadn't been a long wait. The man had very little pure nerve, as he had guessed. The splintering of broken branches continued as he moved forward, then ceased abruptly.

Mark paused. Caution took over control of him again. There was the chance that the other had decided to stand

and fight, had found his courage again, and was reloading the Winchester, improving his position. He stood there, absolutely still for the best part of half a minute, then made to move forward, and at that moment there was the unmistakable sound of hoofbeats on the soft earth.

Swiftly, without pausing to think, he plunged back towards the trail, burst out into the open just in time to see the figure of the bushwhacker, crouched low over the neck of his mount, spurring it on along the trail. Mark brought up the Colts and fired swiftly, but the other was out of sight, and the shots whined harmlessly over his head.

He ducked back and caught up the horse, pulled it the full length of the trail, then climbed up swiftly into the saddle, thrusting the Colts back into their holsters. He doubted the wisdom of trying to hunt down the other, now that darkness was falling rapidly. Within minutes it would be completely dark, and he knew from the spots of blood that were visible on the trail that he had hit the other.

Another thought ran through his mind as he raked spurs over the sorrel's flanks. He had a job to do; to protect that herd on the north pasture. It was just possible that the man who had tried to kill him now wanted him to pursue him, and while he was running out there on the plains, the rustlers would attack the small band of men guarding the herd, and in the morning there would be more cattle gone and possibly more dead men.

Reluctantly he rode out into the open, came down from the hills on to the floor of the canyon. The sun had been down almost an hour now, and the stars were a faint powdering of silvery haze stretching over his head, down to the horizon in every direction. Directly overhead the Milky Way showed clearly, running like a stream of silver across the prairie of the sky.

The night air, cool and refreshing, swept down from the north, sighing down the pine-covered slopes of the mountains, clearing the air of the day's heat and dust. To the east there was a faint yellow glow in the sky where the moon was rising. The open plain around him was quiet now, with a deathly hush, in which nothing seemed to move, and it was as if he were all alone in the world, isolated and cut off from everyone. It was a feeling he had grown used to over the long, weary years and months. Half a mile further on he paused and studied his situation in the flood of moonlight that now covered everything. Round and full, the yellow-white face of the moon had lifted itself clear of the horizon now, sailing majestically into the black vault of the heavens, giving him enough light to see by – a rustler's moon, he reflected idly.

Somehow, he had the feeling that maybe Cal Ventner was right. If the rustlers were going to make another try for some of his beef, this was the perfect night for it.

Ahead of him, as he came out of the canyon which ran along the edge of the hills, it opened up into darker country. Here he crossed the river he had forded earlier. The river was born in the high reaches of the hills, and at this point it was narrow and shallow, but swift flowing, creamy water bubbling over rocks. He felt the current break against the horse's legs, felt the animal struggle and slip on the treacherous rocks underfoot. Then they were over and he gave the sorrel its head.

Silence crowded round him from all sides, a silence born of the vast desert that lay to the west, unseen, but making its presence felt in many small ways; a silence made more intense by the cold light of the moon that flooded over everything, touching the hills and bushes of the country with a stark light, monochromatic and hard on the eye. Once or twice he heard the plaintive crooning of night hawks, and all the time he kept his eyes open for the first sign of a fire, which he knew would be the first inkling he would have of the whereabouts of the camp.

Half an hour later he topped a low rise, saw the long stretch of darker country ahead of him, knew that it was grass, and then he saw the vast shadow of herd bedded down for the night, an irregular, almost circular blotch on the lighter background of the pasture.

To one side, just visible, he made out the tiny spark of orange light that marked the position of the fire. He turned the sorrel's head and rode towards it. Two guards were circling the rim of the herd, singing softly as they rode to keep themselves awake through the long hours, and to combat the loneliness that came to a man in the middle of the night with only the restless cattle to keep him company.

There were two men seated at the fire as he rode up out of the moonlight. In the flicker of the orange firelight, he made out their faces as they stared up at him. Out of the corner of his eye he saw that one of them had pulled his gun from its holster, that the barrel was lined up unwaveringly on his chest.

He forced himself to relax in the saddle, deliberately crossing his arms in front of him, leaning forward a little.

'Relax,' he said softly, evenly. 'I ain't aiming to make trouble. But Ventner seems to reckon there might be some during the night. That's why he sent me here, just in case there is.'

The other remained unconvinced. The gun was still laid on his chest, the barrel had not moved a single inch.

'Don't try any tricks, stranger. Just who are you, and what are you doing here?'

Mark grinned faintly.

'The name's Farrell, Mark Farrell,' he said quietly. 'Ventner hired me yesterday. Seemed to figure that there might be some *hombres* in Mason Bend aiming to make trouble for him. Had a brush with one of 'em on the trail back there, tried to bushwhack me in the timber.'

Slowly the man lowered his gun, glanced sideways at his companion for a moment, then said jerkily: 'Better step down from your horse, mister, take a bite to eat. We weren't expecting company, but you're welcome to anything we got here, specially as you say you're now on the payroll.'

Thankfully, Mark slid from the saddle, turned the sorrel lose and sank down on the soft ground beside the fire. He felt the warmth come at him, driving out a little of the chill coldness of the night. The other scooped some bacon and beans on to a tin plate and held it out to him.

Meanwhile the man seated on the other side of the fire stared at him with an open curiosity, the firelight glinting off the bowie blade of his knife.

'I've heard of you, Farrell,' he said at last in a harsh voice. 'Why would a man like you sign up with an outfit like this?'

'Maybe that's my business.' Mark lifted his head and stared straight at the other, eyes narrowed a trifle. He held the other's gaze for a long moment. It was plain that the other man considered himself to be a tough one, even where a man like Mark Farrell was concerned, a man ready to face up to and answer any challenge.

Mark tightened his lips. No doubt the other man's imagination had provided him with plenty of battles, in which, in fancy, he had taken on outlaws single-handed and destroyed them, emerging victorious. But now, perhaps for the first time, he found himself facing a real challenge and he wasn't at all sure how to go about it. Mark could see him struggling inwardly with his courage, knew that the man had his pride and was wanting to uphold it in front of his companion, that he had started something and he would either have to go through with it, or back down there and then. Suddenly he lowered his gaze, looked down at the blade of the bowie knife, turning it over and over in his hands.

'All right, so it's your business,' he said finally. 'But where do you fit in on the payroll? The boss signed you up as a professional gunman?'

Mark tightened his lips, then laughed mirthlessly.

'Something like that.' He wiped the plate clean with a hunk of bread, thrust it into his mouth and chewed reflectively on it for a moment before washing it down with the coffee.

'Seems to me you need someone around who knows how to handle a gun, and who ain't scared to face up to killers like the Carsons.'

He saw the furrow that appeared on the man's forehead at the mention of the Carson gang, knew that the other had been turning things like that over in his mind for sometime without actually showing it.

'You reckon they may make a try for the herd tonight?' It was the other man who spoke this time, his voice pitched a little higher than before.

'They might. It's the night for it.' He jerked a thumb towards the moon, then towards the dark shadows of the steers milling around three hundred yards away.

He felt the tenseness come to the others, nodded almost imperceptibly to himself. These were hard men who worked at a hard game. Men who had, naturally, to be hard to stay alive, working for a hard boss – but this was different. Here they faced up to men who were forcing the situation to a showdown.

'You reckon that you might be able to stop them if they do?'

'With your help – yes.' Mark locked his gaze with the other's once more. 'Or do you figure on running once they show up?'

He saw the other's head jerk back a little under the deliberate insult, saw the fingers curl more tightly, convulsively, around the handle of the knife, knuckles standing out white with the pressure he was exerting. His whole body was poised, taut and tight. Then he forced himself to relax.

'I don't like you, Farrell,' he said softly, deliberately,

spacing every word carefully. 'I want you to remember that.'

'I'll remember,' Mark promised. He got to his feet. 'But for the moment there's plenty of work for us to do.' Some strange inner sense told him that for the time being there was no danger from the other. In the future, perhaps – but not just now.

'They may try to stampede the herd if they see we mean business, and they realise that we intend to fight them,' said Mark slowly, standing inside the ring of darkness that stood on the outer rim of the firelight. He surveyed the herd closely. They were restless in the moonlight and it would not be a difficult thing to do to stampede them.

Funny, he thought, how moonlight always had that effect on steers. Good-tempered during the day, they could turn into mean, vicious and spiteful creatures once the full moon came up. And there was something else, something that was equally difficult to find an explanation for, the way these creatures always got to their feet at midnight, turned, and then bedded down again.

The yellow moon climbed high into the heavens. The night grew cold and Mark pulled up the high collar of his jacket around his neck. The two men rode in from around the perimeter of the herd. They eyed Mark curiously as he explained why he was there, then nodded slowly at his warning of trouble, almost as if they had been expecting it.

They ate their meal wearily, sitting hunched over the fire as if to draw as much warmth as possible from those flickering flames, pausing every now and again to throw a swiftly apprehensive glance to the north, the direction from which the Carsons would come if they intended to try to move some of this herd that night.

Mark smiled grimly to himself, sitting in the saddle, keeping well into the shadows around the camp. It wasn't easy for these men, he knew, waiting for death to come. There had been times himself, riding under Jeb Stuart during the war, when he had moved into a stretch of desert land that had looked as innocent and deserted as that which lay to the north just beyond the tumbled rocks and crags. In those days, with every mile they rode, death had been a constant companion, riding close.

Here, in this stretch of green pasture, even though the war had been over for many years, he felt that death was equally close, could come to them at any moment. That was why he had to make these men stay awake, keep their eyes open.

Normally, two would ride herd while the other two slept. That way they would get some sleep during the night, but now he meant to keep them awake, all four of the, until first light, when he judged the danger would have diminished.

Mark felt the muscles draw tight just beneath his ribs. Inwardly, he wished that it was not moonlight, that the cold, yellow light were not so bright. It meant they were silhouetted against it, while the gunhawks could move in on them among the rocks and remain unseen.

Midnight. The great herd stirred. It was like watching the dark sea come alive, a rippling motion, sinuous and tremendous, as the three thousand beasts stirred and heaved themselves on to their feet.

A shot bucketed out of the night, shattering the stillness like the lash of a bullhide whip, the splash of flame visible among the rocks.

Mark did not hear the hum of the bullet, knew the moment that gun had been fired that the bullet had not been intended for anyone in the camp. It had been meant only to start these beasts stampeding.

A steer snorted loudly near the edge of the herd. The sound was taken up by the others, all of the animals awake now.

There was no need for him to warn the other men. Each man had recognised the danger to the herd the minute those ringing echoes died away among the dark rocks.

Swiftly, ignoring the herd for the moment, Mark kneed his mount forward, skirting around the camp, heading for the rocks. He saw another flash of flame from a gun muzzle, drew his own guns and fired. The Colt flared again, spitting fire and death into the rocks. He saw the men, crouching low, their heads and shoulders hunched forward as they rose up out of the shadows and ran back to where their mounts stood waiting. One swift leap carried the sorrel clear over the outer fringes of rocks and then he was bearing down on one of the men.

The other must have realised the danger that rode at his back for he suddenly threw a swift glance over his shoulder, then veered off, away from where the horses were, heading deeper into the rocks where it would not be possible for the sorrel to penetrate.

Out of the corner of his vision Mark saw the other men reach their mounts, throw themselves into the saddle and head out, back in the direction of the herd. He let them go for the moment, fired as he rode the other man down, saw him reach an upthrusting boulder and try to heave his way over it, fingers clawing for the top, slipping on the smooth surface. For a moment he stood there on tiptoe, arms upstretched to their fullest extent, striving to get a grip on the rock. Then the slugs tore into him and he fell back, slumping on to the hard ground.

Swinging the sorrel round, Mark headed back for the herd. The four cowboys had their guns out and were firing at the attackers. More guns splashed flame as bullets sang into the night. Again and again – firing and reloading, spinning lances of flame into the darkness that lay all around.

Two of the Ventner men were on the far side of the

herd now, desperately trying to turn them as the steers threatened to stampede along the pasture, back towards the long stretch of canyon that lay to the south. Mark gave them no second glance. They had their work cut out with what they were doing. Best to leave them to it and concentrate on his own job – that of stopping these outlaws who were swinging in on the herd now, shooting off their guns, yelling hoarsely at the top of their voices.

A hundred yards; swiftly Mark closed the distance. Nothing on four legs could equal the speed of a cow horse at that distance. His feet found the stirrups, his legs clung to the sorrel's flanks, and for long moments horse and rider became as one.

He made no attempt to guide the horse now. It knew exactly what was wanted of it. Some hidden instinct that guided man and beast as they rode down on the gunhawks, shadows in the flooding moonlight.

Shots sounded in ragged, uneven rhythm. Swiftly Mark lined his gun on one of the men, drew his aim and squeezed the trigger. The crash of the shot sounded in harsh counter to the bellow of the steers as they began to thunder forward, no longer milling around now in their frenzy, but following the natural leaders as they began to move in one direction. This was what he had feared. These men were not interested now in simply rustling part of this herd. They intended to move off the whole lot, maybe even try to drive them clear to the border once they got rid of the men who had been guarding them.

He saw the man he had fired at suddenly reel in his saddle, clutch at a torn shoulder, then miraculously keep his balance, clinging on to the reins with both hands, having dropped his gun. The mount under him bucked and reared, then turned and fled for the hills in the distance. Two men gone, thought Mark grimly; only the remaining three to take care of.

He turned his head swiftly, looked about for them, saw

to his surprise that they were no longer riding down on the herd, that they had decided not to stay and mix things with this man who could shoot them down with ease. They were spurring their mounts after the wounded member of the party, riding fast into the shadows, cutting away from the stampeding herd.

Riding forward, Mark saw one of the men slipping sideways in his saddle, one foot slipping from the stirrup, one hand grabbing hard at the horn. Then the man's fingers began to slip and loosen, and he half fell around the horse's knees. Mark rode in, leaned low from the saddle and grabbed at the man's jacket, heaving him upright. He lifted and urged the sorrel forward, half-carried, half-dragged the wounded man out of the way of the maddened beasts in the herd, then released his hold, saw the other sink to the ground, safe from those lashing hoofs. There was no time at the moment to check on how badly the man had been wounded. They had to get that herd calmed down, driven back into the pasture, before they broke out and scattered over half of hell and all of creation.

Swiftly he sent the sorrel racing forward, his gun out, firing and cursing at the frightened cattle as they plunged and swerved. When he had emptied his gun, he lashed at the cattle nearest him with the coiled riata, slashing their faces, seeking to build up a wave at the very head of the running columns, a heaving wave that would hold the pressure for a little while, slow down the mighty thunderous herd coming up behind.

Once they could turn the leaders, once they were able to form a crescent there at the head of the sweeping column, thousands of tons of beef and savagery, it ought to be possible to turn them back on themselves, swing the tips of the crescent inward, reforming the milling circle. But it was not going to be so easy with so few men. Fortunately, the others knew their job intimately, these were the men who had been born and bred for this work, like the horses they rode. Nowhere would it have been possible to find a better combination. But it was slow and tiring work.

The men who had started the stampede had been forgotten. They might have been hiding out there in the rocks, waiting for a chance to move in again and complete the job they had begun, once they figured that the time was ripe for just such a move, but Mark did not pause to think of that. Time enough to meet that danger if and when it presented itself. At the moment they had no time to think of anything but getting this herd back into a circle.

A bunch of bawling steers broke loose from the main mass of rippling shadow, went stampeding across the prairie like part of the spoke of a wheel that had suddenly disintegrated. Mark scarcely noticed that they had gone. There was no chance at the moment of going after them, they had to keep with the main portion of the herd.

Slowly, infinitely slowly, over minutes that were dragged out into long, tiring eternities, the tips of the crest that had been formed at the front of the plunging, roaring herd began to close, to move in towards each other as the men edged the crazed animals back on each side.

Mark drilled his heels against the flank of the sorrel. Steers went down and were trampled underfoot by the mighty hoofs that followed. Reloading swiftly, Mark fired at the face of one of the lead steers, saw the animal drop in its tracks. Horns raked the side of his leg as he edged his mount closer, yelling himself hoarse, but he scarcely noticed it.

Another smaller bunch thundered off into the darkness, but they were the last. Gradually the horns met. The stampede had been halted, but it was not all over yet. The herd was still restless, still bawling with its mighty throat, hoofs pounding in the dust, lifting it in a choking cloud that worked its way into Mark's nostrils and mouth so that every breath was an agony and it was almost impossible to swallow.

Now the circle was complete. They had stopped the onward plunge of the steers and gradually worked them back to the pasture. Around and around the rippling mass churned, but the herd had run itself out, it gradually lost its momentum, bunched and crowded together, the animals bedded down again for the night.

Mark let his breath go in a long, whistling sigh that rasped from his lungs and parched, dust-lined throat. He drooped forward a little in the saddle as he rode back to the camp.

The wounded man was there now, had managed to get back to the fire, was seated in front of the flickering flames, his face drawn and tight. He stared up at Mark as the other slid from the saddle and walked forward.

'Reckon you saved my life, mister,' he growled. 'Reckon you saved all our lives.'

'Any sign of those coyotes?' Mark asked sharply.

The other shook his head.

'Last I saw of 'em they were hightailing it into the hills. I doubt if they'll come back tonight.'

'I shot one of them back in the rocks yonder and another in the shoulder.' He squatted beside the other, noticed the blood staining the front of the man's shirt. 'I'll take a look at that wound of yours, and then find that gunhawk out there in the rocks. We may be able to discover who he was.'

The bullet had ploughed deep into the man's shoulder, seemed to be lodged close to the bone. Fortunately the bleeding had almost stopped, but Mark knew that they would have to get that bullet out and as soon as possible. He heaped more wood on to the fire, waited for it to blaze up, his face tight in the red light. Taking his knife from his belt, he laid it down beside him, eyed the other speculatively.

'The slug is still there,' he said flatly, tonelessly. 'I'll have to dig it out. Got any whiskey around?'

'There's a bottle in the saddlebag over there.' The other spoke through clenched teeth, jerked a thumb in the direction of the gear which had been laid out on the edge of camp.

His eyes were wider than usual, but he said nothing more, merely continued to watch Mark as he got to his feet and went over to get the bottle. He came back, held it up to the firelight. It was more than half-full, and he nodded to himself, satisfied. It was the best he could do in the circumstances. Not that the whiskey would dull the pain much, but it made an excellent antiseptic when there was nothing else available.

The man's eyes dropped to the knife as Mark placed it on the ground with the blade in the fire. There was the sound of a rider approaching, and a moment later one of the herders rode in, dropped wearily from the saddle and came up to the fire.

'Maler and Jess are watching the herd,' he said quietly, sinking down to the ground, holding out his hands to the fire. 'They'll be all right now so long as those gunhawks don't hit us again before first light.'

Mark nodded, said nothing. He knew the other was scrutinizing him closely, watching him, trying to form some opinion of him, puzzled a little.

Finally the man said: 'Reckon that I owe you an apology, Farrell. I had you figured wrong. We lost maybe a hundred head, but without your help we might have lost the whole herd and our own lives into the bargain.'

'Are the other two OK?'

'Yeah. Those rustlers were too busy trying to stampede the herd, they took little notice of us.'

'Your friend here has a slug in his shoulder. I'm going to try to get it out for him. Think you could help me?'

The other pushed himself to his feet and came over,

knelt beside the wounded man. Mark held out the whiskey bottle.

'Better take a slug of this,' he suggested. 'It'll help a little.'

Gratefully, his fingers trembling a little, the man took the bottle, tilted it to his lips and gulped the raw spirit, choking on it as it went down his throat. A little ran down his lips and over his chin and Mark took the bottle away.

Pulling back the man's shirt, Mark examined the wound closely. He judged that the slug had gone straight in – and if that were the case, it would help a lot, would mean that he wouldn't have to spend any time fishing for it.

'You ready?' he asked, looking down at the other.

The man compressed his lips into a tight line, then nodded. There was a look of apprehensive fear at the back of his eyes, and Mark motioned to the man beside him to move forward and hold down the other's shoulders. Reaching back, he took the knife from the fire, then picked up the whiskey bottle and doused the wound liberally with the raw liquor. The man on the ground shuddered convulsively, his back arched in spite of the strength of the man holding him down.

Mark went to work expertly. He was no doctor, but for men who rode the trail alone, this kind of knowledge came naturally over the years. They became moderately proficient in bone-setting and digging out slugs.

Working as quickly and as gently as he could, he dug down for the slug, having only the knife to work with. The man moaned low in his throat, then he was quiet and his head slumped loosely to one side, eyes closed. Mark breathed a little easier at that. The other had fainted. In the circumstances it was the best thing that could have happened for both of them. It meant the man would feel no pain until he came to, when it would be all over; and he himself could work more quickly, knowing that the other would feel nothing. Sweat formed on his forehead, even though the night air was cold on his face. Twice he paused and blinked the sweat out of his eyes, then went back to work again.

Half an hour later the tip of the knife blade touched something hard and solid. Gently he eased it out, dropped it on to the ground beside him.

'That's it,' he said tightly, exhaling slowly. 'I'll bandage him up and, apart from a stiff shoulder, he ought to be all right in a couple of weeks. Lucky it didn't smash the bone.'

Finishing the bandaging, he slipped the knife back into his belt, got wearily to his feet, went over to the cook pot over the fire and dug out a slice of beef, chewed it slowly and thoroughly before letting it slide down his throat.

'I'll make some more coffee,' said the other man. He threw his companion a swift glance, then picked up a blanket and draped it over him before going back to the fire.

The smell of coffee on the air made Mark realise just how tired he was. That tussle with the stampeding herd, followed by this episode, had taken more out of him than he had reckoned. He sipped the hot coffee slowly, finally draining the cup. Glancing at the moon, drifting high in the south, he estimated there were still another three hours before dawn.

'Reckon I'll turn in,' he said quietly, getting to his feet. 'I don't figure the Carson gang will attack again tonight.'

'I'll keep an eye on Yacey here,' nodded the other. He hunched himself forward, crouching low over the fire, his eyes fixed on the unconscious man near him.

Mark eyed them closely for a moment, knew there was nothing more he could do there, and went over to where the sorrel stood, pulling his bed roll down, spreading the blanket on the hard ground. Stretching himself out, he stared up at the dark heavens for a long moment, the sound of the herd in his ears; soft and calm now, unlike the raging turmoil of noise it had made a little while before.

Far off, he could hear the mournful crooning of the two cowboys who rode herd, circling the sleeping animals slowly, singing the old songs of the west to keep themselves awake through the long hours – for there was no way of telling when danger and death might strike again.

When he awoke it was still night, but down in the east there was a faint flush of light, heralding the early dawn. He rolled out of his blanket, stretched his weary limbs, and went over to the fire. It had burned down now almost to grey ashes, and the man who sat in front of it was nodding, eyes closed.

Mark put on the coffee pot again, then went over to where the wounded man lay under the blanket. He examined the wound, nodded to himself in satisfaction. There had been very little additional bleeding through the night, and it seemed to be healing properly.

After breakfast he went out into the tumbled heap of rocks which lay on the northern edge of the pasture. The man he had shot down that night still lay there at the base of the huge boulder he had attempted to climb. Mark went forward on foot and turned him over with his toe. The face that stared up at him was one he did not recognise. Black-bearded with wide staring eyes that looked sightlessly at the sun.

Either he had been mistaken and the Carson brothers had not been in that gang of rustlers, or this was one of the two men who rode with them. In Mason Bend he heard that there were five men in the band, the three Carsons and two others.

His lips twisted into a bitter grin as he stood there watching the other for a long moment. At least this meant there was one less outlaw to contend with when it came to the real showdown.

Climbing back into the saddle, he rode to the camp.

The wounded man had come to now, was sitting up, his shoulder stiff under the bandage. He managed a weak smile as Mark came forward.

'You sure fixed my shoulder fine, mister,' he said, nodding. 'You figgering on staying around here for a while?'

Mark hesitated, then shook his head. 'I guess you should be safe enough today. I'd like to ride into Mason Bend and have a word with the sheriff there. Seems he ought to be told about what happened last night. If he doesn't want to do anything about it, then he may have to be forced into it. Seems he's just foolin' most of the townsfolk there, those who elected him into office. Maybe they ought to know something about what's goin' on around these parts.'

'Don't reckon you'll get much help from them,' grunted the man harshly. He moistened his lips. 'Besides he didn't really get himself elected sheriff. He just stepped in and took the job when the old sheriff died. Seems nobody thought to question him at the time.'

Mark nodded his head slowly, eased the Colts in their holsters. He sat quite still in the saddle, leaning forward a little, eyes narrowed and speculative.

'Guess it's about time somebody did question it – pronto,' he said softly. There was something hard and dangerous in the way he spoke, something that both men felt and wondered at.

He sent his horse forward, riding out of camp, heading into the rough country to the north. The trail into Mason Bend lay a couple of miles beyond the outer perimeter of the Ventner spread, and once he hit that trail it would lead him all the way into town.

There was the smell of dust in his nostrils as he cleared the rocks, swung right along the broad trail. The first sun was high above the tops of the pines which, in places, reached down to the edges of the trail. Half a mile ahead it opened out into a wide plain, and he was able to make out Mason Bend on the skyline.

Occasionally he passed a small cattle trail that led off the main track and once, as he was riding between towering, rocky walls, he heard the muted thunder of hoofs in the distance, coming nearer, and five minutes later the stage passed him as he drew in to the side of the trail. The driver and man riding shotgun stared at him curiously as they went past in a cloud of choking white dust. Then the stage had gone, out of sight around the bend in the track, and he turned his face towards the rising sun again, kept it in his eyes all the way into Mason Bend.

The town was at the eastern end of a large plateau, a tableland of hard, rocky ground, and even in the sunlight it held a harsh, inhospitable look. The houses and shops, saloons and stores were all crowded together, fronting on to the main street, a double row of buildings, with others scattered at their back. A small street intersected the main trail through the town, and where they met, in the small square, the bank, two saloons and the only hotel in Mason Bend faced each other at the four corners.

There were few people on the street as he rode into town, the brim of his hat pulled low over his eyes, shading his face from the curious glances.

CHAPTER 4

THE BITE OF
THE RATTLER

Sheriff Colman looked up at Mark as he entered the office, eyeing him with an unexpected show of heartiness. Puffy lowered lids gave his face a sleepy look, but Mark was not taken in by that, knew that although inwardly this man might be a coward, he was also as dangerous as a rattler, ready to strike behind a man's back when he was least expecting it.

He wondered how many men had been shot in the back by this man on the pretext that they were attempting to escape arrest. He guessed that this was the way in which Sheriff Colman preferred to operate. He had the way of talking like that of a man to wayward children, a little too loud and fast and a trifle too friendly.

'I must say I'm sure glad that you came to see me about this,' he said heartily. 'It was the right thing to do, of course. I've heard of these rustlers who've been operating on the range for the past while, mainly on the Ventner spread. But I'm not sure there's much I can do at the moment without any real proof.'

He sat back in his chair, stretched his legs under the

desk and placed the tips of his fingers together, eyeing Mark over them.

'I understand that you've just been signed up on the Ventner payroll.'

'That's right,' Mark nodded. 'I don't aim to be causing any trouble, Sheriff. Maybe this is Ventner's job, but it seems he got no co-operation when he rode into town the other day complaining about these rustlers. He also got jumped on the way back to the ranch. Seems somebody was waiting for him in the canyon and started a rock slide.'

'Now don't you go gettin' riled,' said the sheriff aggrievedly. 'I understand how you feel and all, but it seems to me you ain't really got any right making accusations like this.'

He swivelled away in his chair, not meeting Mark's direct gaze.

'Ventner came here accusing the Carsons, who rode into town some weeks ago. I'll admit they're here, but so far they've caused no trouble, and I ain't got any reason to go arresting 'em like Ventner wants.'

Mark leaned forward over the desk, thrust his face close up against the other's, and said with a dangerous softness: 'Just what d'you mean, I ain't go any right, Sheriff?'

'Now see here, I don't have to go answering your questions.' The other drew back, pushed himself to his feet, knocking the chair over as he did so. 'I'm the law in this town and don't you forget it.'

'You haven't answered my question,' grated Mark. His gaze locked with the others.

In answer, Colman fumbled in the drawer of the desk, rifled through some of the papers there, then pulled one out and laid it on top of the desk. There was a note of triumph in his harsh tone as he said quickly, hurriedly: 'That's your picture, ain't it, Farrell? Wanted for half a dozen crimes in as many states. I can have you arrested right now and thrown into jail until the circuit judge gets here in two months' time. Reckon I'm being soft-hearted in telling you this and giving you the chance to ride out of Mason Bend and keep on riding.'

Sheriff Colman shifted uncomfortably on his feet. Mark controlled his swift rise of temper. 'You figure on doing nothing then, Sheriff?' he asked, tight-reining his voice.

The other glared at him over the desk. 'I'm warning you, Farrell. If you ain't out of town by noon, I'm throwing you in jail and you can do any explainin' you have to, to the judge.'

Mark's eyes, grey and cold, held the other's steadily. He straightened up abruptly, saw the other flinch. There was something here that he didn't quite understand. The sheriff's nervousness, his refusal to arrest him right away once he knew who he was and when he had had the chance, his sudden anger, all of this had roots far deeper than had been uncovered so far.

Mark said stiffly: 'I came here to warn you that rustlers had tried to hit the Ventner herd last night, and that one of them had been killed, and another plugged in the shoulder. If you don't intend to do anything about it, then I'll have to do it myself.'

He whirled on his heel and walked out through the door, leaving the sheriff staring angrily after him, a red flush staining his sallow features.

Mark went out of the office and walked down the street for a block before crossing the track. He kept his eyes alert, watchful for any sudden movement, eyeing the men seated on the boardwalks. He cast about for any sign of the horses which ought to have been tethered in front of the hotel, but the hitching rail was empty, and he guessed that the outlaws were out of town.

Walking over to the nearest saloon, he pushed open the doors and stepped inside. Even at that early hour of the morning the place was full. Men from the hills, prospectors who had made a small strike and were still determined to go on and hit the jackpot, seated at the tables, playing cards with the sharp-eyed gamblers, who were there for only one purpose, to take away the gold dust that these men had won so painstakingly from the rocks of the hills.

Here and there were leaner, stringier men, who wore their guns at their belt. Drovers from the trail, men who rode with the herds that passed through Mason Bend on their way to the railroad back east. After a hard and tiring time on the trail, they usually came here to wash the white alkali dust from their throats.

The saloon was a fancier place then he had expected and somewhat bigger than the size of the town justified. He guessed that it paid off well for the owner, possibly from the prospectors who frequented the place. There was a long bar of smooth, polished mahogany and, behind it, the wide glass mirror which stretched the whole length of the room. At the back of the room there were two larger tables and faro was in progress.

He went up to the bar and rested his elbows on it, watching the players through the mirror in front of him, noticing the taut grim way in which they played, holding their cards tightly, their eyes flicking from side to side, the way all men looked when they gambled their hard-earned money away. Perhaps they knew that the cards had been stacked against them from the moment they joined the game; but it seemed to make no difference.

He ordered whiskey at the bar, drank it slowly. The women there were the kind one usually found in places like this; hard-faced women with bare shoulders, rouged cheeks and bright eyes. They stood around the tables, evidently noticing those men who seemed to have the most money on them.

Draining the glass, he ordered another, stood with it in front of him, watching the bartender as he moved along the bar. There was a man standing at the far end of the bar, shoulders hunched forward, hands curved around his glass, a man with a shock of red hair that showed under his hat, and a hard, cruel face. He seemed to ignore everyone else in the room – everyone except Mark. Every few seconds he would lift his head slightly and watch the other out of the corners of his eyes. It was more than the speculative glance any man gave to a stranger in the town. It was more than idle curiosity.

Mark threw back his head, downed the last of the raw whiskey in a single gulp. It burned momentarily on his tongue. Glancing round, he noticed that the man at the end of the bar had turned, was watching him closely now, his eyes wide and as unblinking as those of a snake.

'You, stranger,' he called suddenly, his voice hard, deep.

Mark paused for a moment before glancing in the other's direction. Then he said quietly, unperturbed: 'You wantin' to say something, mister?'

'Your name Farrell?'

'That's right. What of it?'

Mark waited, every nerve in his body was keyed now, although none of it showed outwardly. But it might have been visible if anyone had looked real close. They would have seen the way he had eased himself a couple of inches from the bar, the way his fingers were thrust out, taut and stiff now, like the branches of a tree, and the manner in which his eyes were watching the other, unfocused, ready to take in every little movement anywhere inside the saloon.

'So you're the *hombre* who's gone to work for Ventner. I wondered what kind of men he'd try to get to work for him. Seems to be scraping the bottom of the barrel, signing on every murderin' sidewinder he can get.'

Mark forced a thin, wintry smile, recognising that the other was thirsting for trouble, ready to meet it the moment it came. Just at that moment he knew that the other was going to blow off his mouth, intended to say why he was doing this. But he did not relax his vigilance for a single second.

'I work for Ventner, if that's what's on your mind,' he said calmly. 'But I don't see that's any business of yours. Not unless you're one of the gunslingers who's riding with the Carsons.'

He saw, from the look that flashed over the other man's face that he had hit the mark. Now everything fell into place. This was one of the men who had tried to rustle that herd during the night, the companion of the man he had shot. He knew now why this man was so eager to kill him.

'How did you guess?' leered the other. He edged away from the bar, his face flushed a little. A grin spread over his face.

'I figured you'd be the only man in Mason Bend, apart from the Carsons, who'd want to get himself killed.'

For an instant the other stiffened, then he took a step forward. Out of the corner of his vision Mark saw that the men in the bar were drifting slowly towards the doors, out of the way of the two men at the bar. Evidently they recognised the signs, he reflected grimly. They would have known this man since he had arrived in town, and possibly they had even heard of his own reputation.

The leer on the gunman's lips widened. Hidden behind his body as he stood sideways to Mark, his right hand had moved slowly and stealthily away from where it had been resting on top of t the bar, was now only an inch above the butt of the gun in his holster. He deliberately held his left hand well away from his belt, hoping to deceive the man who faced him. Clearly he doubted if his draw would be spotted in time, knew that he probably could not outdraw Mark Farrell – and this was the natural situation to surprise a man.

'You seem to be doing a lot of talking, Farrell,' he growled. 'But in this town talk's cheap – as you're going to find out right now!'

Even as he spoke he twisted swiftly on his feet, hurling himself to one side, away from the bar, his right hand flashing down with a blur of speed to the gun at his side, jerking it out of its holster, lining it up with Mark's chest. But there was only one shot fired in the stillness of the saloon, one shot that rang loudly in the confined space, thundering around the bar.

For a moment Clem Hagberg stood there, swaying a little, his arms hanging limply by his sides. Then the gun dropped from his hand and clattered to the floor at his feet as he swayed, striving to hold life in his glazing eyes. There was a look of utter bewilderment on his swarthy features as he slipped to his knees, hovered there for an instant before crashing on to his face.

Almost carelessly Mark pouched the gun from which a wisp of smoke still drifted bluely.

He turned back towards the bar. In one corner of the room, somebody started playing on a tinny piano, the onlookers came drifting back to stare down at the body of the man stretched out on the floor in front of the bar; then the batwing doors were thrust open wide and a harsh voice said authoritatively:

'All right, Farrell. Don't say that I didn't warn you. I've got the drop, so don't try anything hasty. Just unbuckle that belt – with your left hand – and then turn round slowly, keeping your hands where I can see 'em.'

For a second Mark stared at the other, seeking his reflection in the glass behind the bar. The sheriff stood there, a gun in his hand, lined upon Mark's back. He shrugged, lowered his left hand and undid the buckle of the belt, letting it slide from his fingers on to the floor. It would have been sheer suicide to try to draw on the other, even though the idea did cross his mind.

'What's the charge, Sheriff?' he asked quietly, as he turned and faced the other.

'Murder.'

The other came forward, kicked the guns into one corner of the room. 'Now move over to the jailhouse.'

'There are plenty of witnesses here who know that I shot him in self-defence,' said Mark slowly, eyeing the bystanders in the saloon. 'They can testify that he drew on me first.'

'Then they'll get that chance at the trial,' nodded Colman.

He twisted back his thin, bloodless lips, jerked the gun in his hand meaningly towards the door. 'That'll be all, unless you want to try anything.'

Mark glanced from one face to another, watching the men in the saloon, the painted women standing near the tables. He felt their eyes on him, but from the looks on their faces he got the impression that none of them would testify in his defence when the time came. They were afraid. It was simple enough for him to see that; the fear was written in their eyes and on their faces, there for every-one to see; not afraid of Sheriff Colman, but of the Carson brothers, knowing what would happen to them if they did give any evidence that might result in him going free.

He knew it was useless to protest. Maybe all this had been deliberately planned, to frame him. If Hagberg failed to kill him, there was always the chance that some-thing would happen to him in the jail long before the circuit judge got around to Mason Bend on the day of his trial. Going out into the street, he walked in front of Colman across to the jail at the rear of the sheriff's office.

Colman turned the key in the lock and stood back, star-ing at him through the iron bars.

'Reckon you'll be safe enough in there until we've decided what to do with you,' he said softly. There was a look on his face that Mark didn't like, one that boded ill for him.

'I can guess what you mean,' he said thinly. 'You and your friends, the Carsons. You don't mean me to be alive by the time the judge gets here, do you? I'll be shot trying to escape, or maybe you'll start stirring up a lynching mob

– anything so that my death doesn't lie on your conscience.'

'Seems you've decided to take a hand in something that doesn't concern you, Farrell,' said the other. He holstered his gun, surveyed Mark speculatively through the bars.

'I knew about you long before you hit town, but it still don't make sense to me, the way you threw in your lot with Ventner. If you'd played things right, joined up with the Carsons, you'd have been sitting pretty by now, instead of sitting here in this jail. You got something against any of the Carson brothers? That seems the only reason I can think of why you're doing this.'

'Could be you're right,' said Mark tonelessly.

He shrugged his shoulders, deliberately turned his back on the other, and sat down on the metal bunk in one corner of the cell.

The sheriff continued to stand there and watch him for several moments, then turned swiftly on his heel and walked off down the narrow passage.

Mark listened to the sound of his footsteps fading into the distance, heard the heavy door closing at the end of the corridor, then silence.

He sat back on the hard bunk, hands clasped behind his head. When he had ridden into town he hadn't planned on this. He knew very little more now than he had when he had first entered Mason Bend. That one of the Carson brothers had been wounded, he did know. The man he had shot in the saloon hadn't been hit in the shoulder, and therefore he wasn't the man who had been wounded the previous night. He wondered what the sheriff and the Carsons were doing at that moment.

No doubt Colman would waste no time in getting the word to them that he had arrested Ventner's newest and most dangerous hired hand. Then they would have to decide what to do with him. He was far too dangerous to be allowed to live, and yet they wouldn't want to do anything openly. The townsfolk of Mason Bend would ignore a lot, but there was a limit to the murder and rustling that could be done.

Going over to the iron-grille window set high in the wall, he tested the bars with all of his strength. They were set hard in the stone, wouldn't budge a single inch. There was no way out that way, unless someone came along to bust him out of jail, looping a riata around those bars and tying the other end to the saddle of a horse. That way there was always a chance – but as yet no one on the Ventner spread knew that he had been arrested, no one would think of coming to look for him until the next day, and by that time it might well be too late.

Some time during the afternoon Sheriff Colman came back along the narrow passage, rattled his keys in the lock, the Colt balanced in his right hand, the look in his eyes saying quite clearly that he wished Mark would try something and give him the necessary excuse for shooting him down in cold blood. He brought in the tray and the pot of coffee, laid them down on the floor, then stepped back, eyes wary.

'Better eat up,' he said mirthlessly. 'The town's getting real stirred up out there. Seems that guy you shot was pretty well liked around here. The townsfolk don't like strangers riding into Mason Bend and shooting down folk in the saloon.'

Mark twitched back his lips into a faint, wry grin.

'That's just what I was figuring might happen. Who's out there stirring 'em up? The Carsons? That *hombre* in the saloon was Clem Hagberg, one of the killers who bust out of jail in Dodge with the Carson brothers – and you know it, Sheriff.'

For a moment he saw the fear at the back of the other's eyes, saw the man's gaze slide away. Mark gave him a long, cool glance.

'Just why are you doing this, Sheriff?' he asked softly. 'Scared of 'em – or have they promised you a share of the loot they got stached away somewhere?'

'You talk too much,' snarled the other viciously.

His hand hovered over the gun at his hip and Mark knew that it would take very little to make him use it, unless Bart Carson had given orders that he was to be kept alive until he came along.

'If I were you, I'd watch what I say. That crowd out there are getting all steamed up over somethin' and I reckon I know what it is. More of them in the saloon, and once they're lickered up, they'll try to take the law into their own hands, and there'll be a lynching.'

'And, of course, as sheriff here, you'll do everything in your power to see that nothing happens to the prisoner, and that he gets a fair trial once the circuit judge gets here.'

There was sarcasm in Mark's tone as he stared at the other through the bars of the cell. He grinned.

'Reckon you people have some funny laws in this town that allow killers like the Carsons to go about scot free, plundering, killing and rustling. How long do you figure the ordinary citizens are going to stand for it? Someday they'll discover what's going on and then your life ain't going to be worth a plugged nickel.'

Fear came back with a rush into the sheriff's eyes. For a moment he stood there looking in at Mark. Then he pulled himself sharply together, said with a growing confidence: 'You ain't going to be allowed to see that day if it ever comes, Farrell. You can be sure of that.'

He went off down the passage, slammed the door at the other end. Mark ate the food slowly. He had no appetite, but he knew that he had to eat, that there might be a chance for him before the mob hit the jail, and he would have to be ready to take it if it came.

Deep down inside he wondered what kind of end Bart

Carson had in hand for him. He still couldn't know the real reason for his interest in him, could never have connected the death of the girl in the stage hold-up with the man who had set himself up against him here.

He finished the meal, drank the lukewarm coffee and settled himself back on the bunk, listening to the sounds outside. It was hot inside the cell, the air still and filled with dust that came filtering in through the barred window. In the distance along the street he could hear the sound of voices, interspersed occasionally by shots, and guessed that the crowd were still in the saloon, with the drinks being paid for by Bart Carson.

He doubted if any of the ordinary citizens of Mason Bend would take part in any lynching; but it was always easy to find a host of roughnecks willing enough to carry out a hanging, provided they got well paid for it, well liquored up.

He dozed for a little while, and when he woke again the shadow on the wall told him that the sun was already westering. There was a coolness in the cell now, but outside the shouting and the shooting still went on. Bart Carson would be waiting until sundown, he figured, before he made any play.

He pushed himself upright, sat on the edge of the bunk. There was the sound of a solitary rider moving down the street outside. The street was coming to life now that the heat of the early afternoon had lessened. Some of those people out there were decent citizens, men and women who had come out here from back east, seeking a place where they and their children might live in peace, start new lives without fear of sudden death and violence. But so far such things were hard to find. The lawless element was always there, ready to pounce, an element represented by such men as the Carsons.

He himself seemed to have walked right into a hornet's nest, and certainly he was in the toughest spot of his entire career. Without a gun in his hand, he was helpless. He got to his feet, tried the window once more, pulled with every bit of strength in his body, then gave it up. He sat back on the bunk, unsettled inside.

Slowly the shadow on the wall crept around and, outside, it grew darker as evening approached. Still no sign that Carson was ready to make his play. There were still sharp cries in the distance, the growing mutter of people, of voices swelling in anger.

What lies the Carsons would tell to get the people on their side, he did not know, but what did it matter so long as they were believed, if only for one night. After that it would make little, if any, difference. A wanted killer would have been taken from the jail and hanged. That was all there was to it. Ventner might try to protest, but he would get nowhere and it would not be long before he, too, was finished.

He cursed himself silently for ever having fallen into this trap. He ought to have realised that there was a plan being built up against him the moment he had ridden into town. There had been that rider who had tried to bushwhack him when he had ridden out to the north pasture. Evidently the Carsons had known every move he had made.

'Not be too long now, Farrell.' Colman had come back and was standing in the passage just outside the door, a grin on his features. There was an unholy light in his narrowed, deep-set eyes. His tone took on a silky, bantering note.

'Like I said earlier, you ought to have taken my advice and ridden out of town while you had the chance. Now see what you've let yourself in for.'

He laughed harshly, nodded his head. Outside it was almost dark. Mark felt the tightness growing inside him as he stood there. There was the sound of the outer door of the office opening, someone called something in a gruff voice.

Colman turned, stared along the corridor. 'That you, Mister Carson?' he called.

There came a muffled answer from along the corridor, and Colman glanced back into the cell, his hands gripping the bars tightly, lips parted in a vicious grin. 'Reckon they'll be coming for you right soon, Farrell,' he said thickly. 'Then we'll go for Ventner. He won't be able to hold out much longer once you're finished and—'

He broke off suddenly, his voice rising sharply on a grunt of pain. Someone said softly: 'Just hold it there, Sheriff, and you won't get hurt.'

For a long second Mark stood in the middle of the cell, scarcely able to believe his ears. Virginia Ventner's voice!

He went forward quickly. The sheriff stumbled a little to one side and Mark was able to see that Mort Kennedy, the ranch foreman, was standing just a little way behind him, the barrel of his Colt jammed hard into the small of the lawman's back. A moment later Virginia Ventner came into view, plucked the bunch of keys from the sheriff's belt, and began fitting them, one after the other, into the lock, until she found the right one. She swung the door of the cell open.

'Quickly – outside!' she hissed, gesturing him out into the passage.

He stepped quickly through and a moment later, the sheriff, stripped of his guns, was pushed inside, a gag over his mouth, his hands tied tightly behind his back.

Kennedy glanced down for a moment at his handiwork, then nodded satisfied.

'I reckon that ought to hold him long enough, Miss Virginia,' he said quietly. 'We'd better get out of here, fast. That crowd's nearly ready to bust their way in here, and once they find him gone—'

Mark nodded, took the sheriff's guns and slid them into his holsters. He felt more sure of himself now as he motioned the others towards the rear of the jail.

Moments later they were in the narrow alley at the back of the jailhouse. Everything was quiet here, nothing moving in the shadows. A quick look around to make certain, then he motioned the others forward and they slipped soundlessly around the side of the building, edging in the direction of the main street.

In the near distance the yelling and shooting rose to a crescendo. Mark guessed that now it was dark Carson would not want to waste any more time. There was always the chance of interference from the people of Mason Bend, and he didn't want to risk too much trouble with them, not at the moment anyway, until he had the upper hand completely in this territory.

'They'll be moving in on the jail in another couple of minutes,' whispered Kennedy urgently.

Mark nodded.

'Where did you leave the horses?'

'Down the road apiece.' It was the girl who answered. Her voice was calm and quiet and, of the two, she seemed the more relaxed. 'We didn't dare ride them right up to the jail in case anybody started getting a mite suspicious.'

Mark rubbed his chin thoughtfully. He dare not show himself on the street, and yet there was no time to be lost. The crowd in the distance had suddenly grown silent and that was a bad sign. He glanced round at Kennedy.

'Nobody knows you here,' he said quickly. 'Get the horses and bring them here – and hurry!'

The foreman moved out into the street, hesitated a moment, then he hitched his gunbelt a little higher about his waist, stepped forward and was lost to sight.

A host of questions and half-formed thoughts were running chaotically through Mark's mind at that moment, but he knew that they would have to wait for their answers until he and the others were clear of the town.

He waited in the shadows with a growing sense of impatience riding him. He was armed now, it was true, free of that cell, but he knew that he could not hope to shoot down all of the men who would soon be marching on the jail, and with the girl with him, he dared not risk a show-down.

He uttered a faint sigh of relief as Kennedy came back leading the horses.

'Any trouble?' he asked harshly, keeping in to the shad-ows.

The foreman shook his head. 'They're all up there on the steps of the saloon,' he said grimly. 'A big bunch of them. They look ready for trouble, and there are three men talking to them. One of the *hombres* has his arm in a sling.'

The Carson brothers. There was no longer any doubt in Mark's mind as to the identity of the men who were out to kill him.

'Let's get saddled up and get out of here while we have the chance,' he said briskly, stepping up into the saddle of the third mount they had brought with them.

It had obviously been a measure of the crowd's concen-tration on what the Carsons had been saying that they had thought nothing suspicious of a man and a woman bring-ing in an empty mount.

Even though every nerve in his body was screaming silently at him to urge his mount into a gallop, he restrained the impulse, and they let their horses walk slowly to the edge of town. Behind them, just as they reached the blackness of night on the outskirts, they heard the sudden yell that came from fifty throats, the loosing off of gunshots in the middle of town. Then they touched spurs to their horses and hit the trail leading out of Mason Bend, riding swiftly into the night.

How long they had before there was a posse on their tail, Mark did not know, but he felt sure that as soon as the sheriff was discovered, trussed like a fowl in his own cell, Carson would send men after them, trying to cut them off before they hit the Ventner spread.

They followed the trail for half a mile, then swung off into the desert that lay silent on their left. The moon was visible only at brief intervals through breaks in the cloud that came driving in from the west. With the cloud came the rain, a solid blanket of rain that struck them forcibly, rushing in on them out of the darkness.

Mark crouched low over the neck of his mount. At least, he thought grimly, the rain would help in that it would wash away their trail and make it difficult, if not impossible, for the posse to track them. Yet that was a dubious advantage. It would not take Carson long to figure out who could have saved him and there was always Sheriff Colman there to talk. He would know that the only place they could head for with any chance of safety would be the Ventner ranch, and if they pushed their horses hard, they might be able to cut across country and head them off long before they reached the north pastures.

If Virginia Ventner or the foreman thought of this, they gave no outward sign, but urged their mounts forward, heads low against the driving rain.

To the north lightning flared suddenly, a brilliant splash of savage force across the dark heavens. It was followed moments later by the gun roll of thunder, rumbling echoes that spilled over the wide plains.

Peering ahead, Mark pushed his sight through the dimness of driving rain, trying to estimate where they were. He did not doubt that Kennedy knew exactly and for the moment he was content to follow them.

Another flash of lightning. The falling drops of rain, huge and silvered, were held in the sight, caught and frozen in that weird flash of light. Mark blinked his eyes to adjust them to the blackness that followed. More thunder rolled and bucketed around them, crashing from the hills in the distance.

Often he turned, tried to peer behind him, eyes searching for any sign of pursuit, knowing that while the storm lasted his ears would never manage to pick out the sound of men riding hard after them.

Half an hour later the nature of the terrain changed. The hills and crags swept down towards them, hemming them in. Then, as abruptly as it had come, the storm swept past them.

Mark lifted his head, drew in a deep breath. There was a solitary flash of lightning far behind them, touching the crest of the mountains far away, while overhead the clouds had thinned, then vanished altogether, and the sky was clear, with the stars showing brilliantly as if the heavens had been washed clear by the storm and everything was brighter than before. Soon the moon came out behind them, bathing everything in its yellow glow.

At the end of the long, narrow canyon they halted, giving the horses chance to get their wind. The beasts were tired, had made the journey all the way from the ranch into town, whereas those used by any men riding hard on their tail would be fresh.

Sitting tall in the saddle, he listened intently. At first he could hear nothing. A vast and clinging silence seemed to hang like a shroud over everything around them, crushing out all sound. Then he paused, turned slightly, staring out to his right. Downgrade there was the unmistakable murmur of horses moving fast.

Kennedy said impatiently: 'They'll be on us soon. We'll never make it to the ranch in time. Our horses are tired now.'

'They may pass us,' said Mark grimly. He sucked in a harsh breath. 'They're about half a mile away and off the trail. They must have anticipated that we'd cut across country.'

He looked about him, his keen-eyed gaze taking stock of their situation. The rugged boulders of the rocky ground that rose up sheer on either side of them formed a natural barricade.

'Into the rock!' he ordered swiftly. 'Hurry! If the horses keep quiet, we may be safe!'

They urged their mounts into the rocks, guiding them over the smooth, treacherous boulders that littered the way. Not until they were well away from the narrow track was Mark satisfied. Then he slid from the saddle and wormed his way forward, easing the Colts in their holsters.

The riders were coming closer now, seemed to have swerved to head in their direction. A moment layer he saw that he had been only partially right. Carson had decided that they must have reached the point where they would have overtaken them and had decided to split his men. One half was already heading on towards the spread, the others were moving in the direction of the canyon. He cursed softly under his breath as he crouched down, then moved back to the others.

'They've split into two groups,' he murmured tightly. 'If they find us we'll have to fight it out. I reckon that you'd better get further back into the rocks with the horses, Miss Virginia, while Mort and I do our best to hold them off. There can't be more than half a dozen of 'em in this group.'

He saw the girl tilt her chin defiantly. 'I'm not running from them,' she said quietly, in a tone that brooked no argument. 'I've never run from these outlaws yet.' She reached up, took the Winchester from its scabbard, and held it grimly in her hands.

Mark opened his mouth to argue, then caught the foreman's wry glance and knew that it would be useless. Instead, he said quietly: 'You know how to handle that thing?'

She nodded confidently.

'I reckon I'm as good a shot with it as a man.'

'All right, then.' He nodded. 'Let's get ready to meet them, but remember, hold your fire until I give the word. They may miss us altogether, and I don't want to have to take them on unless it's absolutely necessary. There's always the chance that the other group may hear gunfire and come hightailing it back here, and then we're finished.'

They edged forward, crouched down in the long shadows thrown by the tall, upthrusting boulders, weapons ready. In the moonlight, it was now possible to make out the riders as they came on, spurring their horses cruelly. There were seven of them, Mark saw, and he recognised the man who led them, tall and familiar. Bart Carson, one of the men he had sworn to kill. He felt something tighten in him and he thumbed back the hammers of the Colts, watching as the men came on and, in spite of what he had said earlier, he found himself wishing that they would find them, so that he had an excuse to shoot down Bart Carson.

CHAPTER 5

GUNFIGHT IN SHADOW

The riders swung into the shadow of the canyon, held
their mounts in motion, and Mark saw them sitting high in
the saddle, eyes and heads moving from side to side. He
guessed that they were uneasy, knowing that this was an
ideal place for an ambush, and fearing a bullet at any
moment, the splash of gunfire from the deep, moon-
thrown shadows on either side.

Mark found himself holding his breath, threw a swift
glance sideways to where the girl and Mort Kennedy lay
behind the rocks, their bodies mere humps of shadow just
seen when one knew where to look for them. He doubted
if any of the riders down below could see them, but he
knew that it was unwise to take that chance.

The sound of a harsh voice came from below, thinned and
short. It was not easy to see the riders now, they had ridden
into the deep shadow thrown by the tall, rearing rocks on the
far side of the canyon, and he was forced to follow their
progress by the sound of their mounts. He waited tensely, not
sure how near that outfit would come, whether they had
paused down there, staring up into the chequered pattern of

moonlight and shadow, seeking them out.

He grew aware that the men below had stopped. There was the scrape of a horse's hoof on rock, then silence. He could feel eyes watching him, unfriendly eyes, hands hovering nervously close to gun butts, ready to sweep down, jerk up and fire.

It was the moment for quick decision. Whether to wait until they moved out into the light again and open fire, taking the initiative while he still had it, cutting down as many of these men as he could before they gathered their wits and returned their fire, diving for the cover of the rocks. The moment and then the decision was taken for him. From somewhere above their heads there came the loud, harsh whinny of a horse. The sound travelled far in the still darkness, giving their presence there away as clearly as if he had stood up and shown himself to the men below.

A sudden yell from the canyon floor, the sound of horses being urged among the rocks. Then the stabbing flashes of gunfire and the slugs whining off the rocks near by, with the shriek of tortured metal.

He fired back, sighting at the muzzle flashes, unable to see the men. Among the rocks a man yelled loudly in sudden agony, and he knew that one of his slugs had found its mark.

Virginia Ventner was firing steadily, too, with the rifle, resting it on the boulder in front of her, squeezing off her shots slowly and with care. He threw a quick glance in her direction, noticed with a feeling of pleased surprise that she had not exaggerated when she had claimed to be as good a marksman with the rifle as any man. He need not have worried about her on that score, he thought, but they were still not out of trouble.

He glanced down again and at that moment he caught the sudden movement out of the edge of his vision, the dark shadow that went slipping away among the rocks to their right, head down, moving quickly, scrambling from one concealing boulder to the next.

The distance was less than a hundred feet, and he knew that if the other managed to work his way around them, to come out at their backs and fire down on them from above, they were finished. Here they had cover from the men in front of them, but they were exposed to any fire from their rear.

He loosed off another couple of shots down the slope, then wriggled away into the rocks, reloading the guns as he drifted forward, watching the spot where the gunman had vanished. Virginia and the foreman would have to take care of the others for the moment, he decided. This man represented a far greater danger if he wasn't stopped in time.

Very carefully he made his way up the rocks, snaking from one narrow defile into another, moving like a cat in spite of the stiffness in his aching limbs. Several times he was forced to halt for breath, and it was while he was crouching in a narrow space between two boulders that he heard the other man, very close, less than a dozen feet away. He seemed to be far less cautious than he ought to have been, and several times Mark could make out the sharp, metallic clash of his sixes as they struck the hard rock.

When the other paused, he edged forward again, eyes alert. Here there were fewer shadows in which to hide and several minutes passed before he came out of a narrow gulch and spotted the gunman less than four feet below him, snaking towards the edge of the rocks, bringing up his Colts to line them up on the girl below.

For a moment the other paused, turning his head this way and that, and Mark guessed that the gunhawk had possibly made out Kennedy's shape lying behind the rocks down below, but could see no sign of him, and he was puzzled and a little worried. The man had chosen that particular spot with care. From there he commanded an excellent view of the whole stretch of the rocky ground below, could have shot down any of them with ease, drilling them in the back.

He breathed a silent prayer that he had seen the man in time, edged forward an inch at a time, steadying himself, slithering down until he was right behind the other.

Pushing the barrel of the Colt into the man's back, he said softly: 'Relax, mister, one wrong move out of you and this gun goes off. I'm just itching for the chance to use it.'

He felt the other stiffen, then release his hold of his gun. It clattered down the rocks in front of him and was lost.

'That's better. I don't know who you are, stranger, probably one of those drovers who hit town today. The Carsons must have talked you into this, probably telling you it was going to be easy, just a case of hunting down a girl and a couple of men.'

'They said you were a killer, Farrell, and I believe them.'

'Maybe so, and you're in the right position to find out. I don't want to have to kill you, but I will if—'

Abruptly the other swung, kicking back with his foot, catching Mark on the shin and taking him completely by surprise. He staggered back and a second later the other's bunched fist caught him on the side of the head, almost tearing his ear off. The gun fell from his hand as he staggered against the rock.

Acting on instinct, he rolled to the side, lowering his head, bending his body into a half-bow. The other's savage kick, aimed for his groin, missed, caught him on the thigh, sending a spasm of agony lancing through his leg. The impact of hitting the rocky wall behind him struck hard on his shoulder blades, knocking all of the wind from his lungs.

Then the other was coming in again, swinging up his booted foot. There was the look of murder on the gunman's face and Mark knew that it was now a battle to the death, that the other would not let up until he had killed him.

The wild kick missed and instinctively he reached out and caught the swinging foot, held on grimly while he fought the tears away from his eyes and sucked air down into his heaving lungs. Then he heaved and twisted with

86

all of the strength of his arms, realising that whatever happened he had to finish this as quickly as possible.

At any moment those other gunfighters might start coming up the rocks to take Virginia and Kennedy from both sides, cutting them down by sheer weight of numbers. And there was always that other group of men to be taken into account. If they picked out the thunder of gunfire, they would immediately head back to help their companions.

The man was scrambling to his feet as Mark blinked his eyes, pushed the hair out of his face, tried to focus on the shadowy figure in front of him. There was a dull ringing in his ears that refused to go away, and he realised that he was half deaf from the effect of that wild haymaker that had just missed his chin.

The drover charged in, feet scraping on the rocks underfoot. He was too confident now, thought that Mark was finished, done for. As he lunged forward, Mark waited, saw the other's arm upraised and drove his fist into the man's unprotected face. With a wild, bleating cry, the other whirled back. Under his bunched fist Mark felt the man's nose squash and blood came, flowing down his face. Still he came in for more, refusing to give up, arms wide, fingers clawed as he sought to throw his arms around Mark, throw him off balance.

Mark dug in his heels and waited. He knew that the other would be a dirty fighter and this time was ready for the man's sudden change of tactics, saw the hand that came lunging for his eyes, fingers stretched straight and rigid, seeking to blind him. The gunman's eyes glittered with the killing fever as he crowded in. Breath came gasping in and out of his lips.

Lowering his head, Mark swung up with a vicious uppercut, having all the time in the world to pick its point of impact on the other's chin. The man gave a shrill sucking gasp of pain, staggered back, arms flailing as he tried to steady himself on the slippery, treacherous surface.

Giving him no time to recover, Mark went after him, driving him back with short, sharp jabs to the face and stomach, vicious, chopping blows that smashed on the other's nose again, spreading more blood over his twisted distorted features. The man grunted loudly, stopped dead. For a second he stood there, trying to lower his hands to defend himself, to ward off some of the piston-like blows that hammered against his body.

Blinking, shaking his head wearily, the man tried to move forward again, but Mark drove into him, lowering his shoulder, using it as battering ram on the man's chest, hurling him back so that his feet actually left the ground and he half flew through the air. Toppling sideways, the other teetered for a second, then uttered a wild, shrill scream of mortal terror as he realised for one fleeting moment that he had moved far too close to the edge of the rocky ledge for safety. For the barest fraction of a second he almost caught his balance. Then he was gone, falling backward, his body bounding sickeningly as it crashed down the rocks, out of sigh, into the moon-thrown shadows far below.

Sharply Mark pulled himself together. His face burned and there was a dull, brutal ache in the rest of his body. A shot whistled close to his head and he ducked swiftly, slithering down a narrow gully, jerking the other Colt from its holster. In a shower of stones he reached the narrow ledge some twenty feet below, dropped down beside the rocks as more lead slammed and ricocheted around him, cutting through the air where his body had been a few moments earlier.

One glance was enough to tell him that the girl was still unhurt, firing slowly and steadily into the shadows below. The brief, stabbing flash of light told him roughly where the rest of the outlaws were. Two bullets struck wide of Mark's position, screamed thinly into the distance with a high-pitched banshee wail. Then another volley crashed down and he was forced to lie low, to keep his head down for long seconds. When he glanced up once more he saw the figures that scrambled forward, cutting nearer through the rocks, less than fifty feet away, working their way up, spreading out in a long line to take them from both sides.

He sucked in a swift breath, aimed and fired in a single reflex movement. One of the men dropped out of sight and did not reappear, but he could not tell from that distance, in the moonlight, whether his bullet had found its mark or not.

Glancing out over the top of the canyon wall on the opposite side of the narrow track, he scrutinised the country that lay beyond, rolling flat and smooth to the distant horizon, seeking that other bunch that had ridden off to the south. As yet there was no sign of them, but that did not mean they were out of trouble, even if they finished the six men below.

The outlaws were closing rapidly now, vaguely seen shadows, fleeting shapes that were visible for scant seconds before they had dived into the shadows once more. Mark lay back and waited, easing his finger off the trigger. It was obvious what those others wanted. They were merely drawing their fire, knowing that soon they would be plumb out of ammunition. Then they would move in for the kill.

'Hold your fire, Kennedy,' he yelled loudly. 'You too, Miss Virginia. They're just trying to make us waste ammunition shooting at shadows. Wait until they get nearer and then make every shot count.'

The other two stopped firing. He saw out of the corner of his eye that Kennedy was reloading his guns, jerking his head up at frequent intervals to check on the advancing men.

From somewhere below a harsh voice yelled: 'If you're up there, Farrell, reckon you'd better throw down your irons and come down here with your hands high. We don't want to have to kill the girl, or that other *hombre*. You're the one we want.'

Bart Carson's voice. He knew it immediately and the mere sound of it tightened the muscles under his ribs, flexing the finger on the trigger of the gun as he sought the location of the other. He could see nothing. For the moment the killers had gone to ground. Maybe they were waiting for Carson to give the signal when they would rush them, he reflected.

'You hear me, Farrell?'

Keeping his head down, he yelled back: 'I hear you, Carson. If you reckon that we trust you, you're mistaken. The minute you show your face we'll blow it off.'

There was a harsh laugh and he tried desperately to guess where the other was hidden, but in the flooding yellow moonlight, hearing was deceptive and he waited with a growing impatience deep within him. He knew that the other was deliberately taunting him, trying to get him to give himself away. Maybe trying to keep his attention while some of the other men moved in closer. He let his gaze wander from side to side, seeking any movement, ready to catch the vaguest shadow.

'You've interfered too much in my plans,' went on the other thinly. 'I don't know what your axe is to grind, or why you threw in your lot with Ventner. But you made a big mistake, and for that I'm going to kill you.'

'Shoot me down, fill me full of holes like you did that woman in the stage?' All the anger, all of the bitterness of the past years came flooding out in his words.

A pause, then: 'What in tarnation you talking about, Farrell?'

The other sounded curious, but that could be a trap, too. Mark swung his gaze slowly, trying to take in everything, then he lifted his head slightly and he knew why Carson had kept on talking like this, why he had wanted to keep Mark's attention on him.

Far out there, in the dull wash of yellow moonlight, he saw the cloud of dust, faint and barely discernible on the wide expanse of the prairie, but coming closer. Too far away for the hoofbeats to be heard, but near enough for him to recognise that it was a bunch of riders; that same bunch that had split from the main group and headed in the direction of the Ventner spread. No doubt that the sound of gunfire had carried over the prairie, no doubt why those men were riding back as fast as they could push their mounts.

'You know exactly what I'm talking about, Carson,' he snapped. 'That stage you and your brothers held up outside Dodge, the woman you shot down before she could get out. That was my sister and when I heard who killed her, I swore I'd find them and shoot them down like the coyotes they are.'

'Yeah.' There seemed to be a new note of awareness in the outlaw's voice. 'So that's it. I might have known it had to be something like that to drive a man to do what you've done. But I reckon it all had to end sometime, and this is where it ends for you.'

Gunfire broke out suddenly and Mark ducked with a sudden oath as slugs crashed within inches of his head. He had been careless, had lifted his head too high, intent on listening to what Carson had been saying, and it had almost been the end of him.

Concussion rocked among the boulders. Beyond the canyon the bunch of riders were approaching swiftly, kicking up dust. It was impossible to see how many there were, but inwardly Mark felt the sinking sensation of defeat. With the other outlaws below them and their horses far up the rocky face of the canyon wall, there was no way out for them. For the first time he recognised the trap into which he had led them.

There wasn't much time for speculation. About ten seconds' delay before the riders entered the boxed-in canyon, joined forces with the rest of the gunmen down below and overwhelmed them by sheer weight of numbers.

The seconds ticked away while they waited for a move from Bart Carson. Mark tried to probe the darkness below him with his gaze, then jerked up his head swiftly as gunfire bucketed through the night. His forehead furrowed suddenly as he realised that the riders, swinging in from the prairie, were firing in the saddle, their guns blazing even before they reached the canyon.

Down below there was a sudden and unexpected movement. Carson's loud and hoarse voice yelled an order. The men with him began to run for their horses inside the canyon. Instinctively Mark brought up his gun and fired at their fleeing figures before they vanished into the deep gloom. Moments later the outlaws burst out of the canyon and spurred their mounts away, keeping to the narrow trail.

Slowly, Mark got to his feet, stared stupidly for an instant as Teeler Malloy, grey-haired, but sitting straight in the saddle, led the rest of the ranch hands into the canyon.

When they had collected their horses and gone down to meet the others, they found a couple of the killers lying among the rocks on the floor of the canyon. Teeler gave them a quick, professional glance.

'They won't be worrying us none,' he muttered briefly. 'Don't reckon there's much point in riding after those other coyotes. They'll have a head start by now.' He cackled loudly. 'Never saw anybody hightailing it outa here so fast in all my life.'

Mark nodded slowly. 'Good thing you happened along, Teeler. We figured you might be that other gang. They split up out there.'

'Ain't seen nothing of any others,' went on the oldster quietly. He stared thoughtfully into the moonlit darkness. 'Could be they'll ride on apiece and then head back. You figure they may try something more tonight?'

'Not tonight.' Mark's tone was decisive. 'They've been whipped and they'll want to bring in more men before they try anything more. But Bart Carson can't stop now. This is a fight to the finish.'

They turned their mounts, rode out into the moonlit plain, heading south, with the wind in their faces. Overhead the stars winked, huge and brilliant, with a polish like diamonds sparkling against the jet of the night. The rain had washed the sky clear of dust and the night air in their nostrils smelled fresh with the scent of the pines in the far distance. Over on their right, as they rode, the mountains on the skyline lifted tall, ragged peaks that caught the moonlight so that they stood out starkly on the horizon.

Mark rode beside Virginia Ventner, occasionally watching her closely out of the corner of his eye. She sat easily in the saddle, her face touched with the moonlight so that part of it was in shadow. In spite of himself, Mark felt a stirring in his body as he rode with her.

Alone – away from women, it had been easy to forget them, to put them out of his mind and concentrate only on the terrible hatred, the need for revenge that had been riding him these years. Easy to do the things he had to do, hunting down those three men he had sworn to kill, easy to ride into small towns along the trail and keep himself out of trouble, ready for anything, alert for any kind of danger. The lonely man who rode the wide country with his eyes on the far horizons, wondering only how far beyond them he would be forced to travel before he met up with the Carson brothers and burned all of the vengeance and revenge out of his system in a blaze of gunfire.

Now, seeing this woman, sensing her nearness, feeling the curious stirring, the singing of his blood in his veins, and behind his temples, it came to him forcibly that perhaps there were more things to life than hunting men like animals, with his mind consumed by the need to slay.

She turned after a while and looked directly at him, and there seemed to be a wondering expression in her eyes, a look which he had never seen on her face before, as if she had suddenly realised something about him which she had not known earlier.

'I heard what you said to that outlaw back there in the rocks, Mark,' she said softly, and her voice held a strange

warmth to it. 'About your sister, I mean. It explained so
many things that had puzzled me about you ever since you
rode into the ranch and asked for a job. I hoped then that
my father would turn you away. Even though common
sense told me that we needed a man like you if we were to
survive, a man with the killer instinct who was not afraid of
these gunmen, and who had killed before. I felt it would
be dangerous to have you around, that you would bring
more trouble with you than you were worth.'

'And you still feel the same way?' He deliberately forced
all emotion out of his tone.

She hesitated, then shook her head very slowly, almost
imperceptibly. 'No. Up to a little while ago, even after we
had broken you out of jail, I still thought you were nothing more than a low-down killer, useful to us only in that
you could stand up to these men and fight.'

He rode in silence for a long moment, aware of her
scrutiny, knowing that she was struggling deep within
herself to adjust her mind to the new ideas, the new knowledge about him.

After a little while, she went on: 'Do you hate me, Mark,
for thinking like that about you?'

'Have I ever said that I did?'

'Not with words. But you look at people, not only me,
but everyone, as if you hated the whole world, as if you're
blaming everyone for what happened all those years ago.'

He nodded. 'I guess that's how I must have felt,
although I may not have realised it. When you lose someone like that and in such a senseless way, you don't seem
to have the capacity for thinking straight any more. All you
want to do is to go out and kill.'

Virginia straightened in her saddle, lifting her shoulders to ease the ache in her back, then edged her mount
closer to his. Her hand came out and rested on his arm for
a moment.

'Somehow, I can't help liking you, Mark. This is something I've never felt before for any man.'

'Do you?'

'Very much.'

'I'm glad.'

The singing excitement was back in his veins and for a moment he forgot the danger which still faced them, forgot everything.

'Those men – the Carsons,' she said quietly. 'Why did they kill your sister?'

He tightened his lips. The illusion was gone, the spell broken. He felt the coldness of the night air on his face.

'Who knows why men like that do anything?' he said harshly. 'There was no need for what they did. She couldn't harm them. They probably thought it was fine sport, killing an innocent woman.'

'And you hate them even now? You still mean to kill them?'

'Yes.' He spoke through clenched teeth. 'Nothing is going to change that. A man has to do what he must.'

'I think I understand.' She gave a little nod, turned her face to the south from where the night wind blew. 'I think I would feel the same if I were in your place.'

They rode into the rocks, the horses picking their way carefully through the tumbled mass of boulders. Here the trail was virtually non-existent. Mark watched the ground closely as they rode through. It might be that if the showdown came they would have to defend the ranch and this place would make an excellent defensive position. His keen-eyed gaze took in the mass of shadow, of moonlight, assessing its value as such a position, calling on his training in the recent war, looking at the ground through the eyes of a cavalryman and not a cattleman.

Here there was a silence which seemed to be built up, rather than broken by the sound of the horses' hoofs on hard ground. The hard grey eyes drifted in every direction, missing nothing. Not even the slightest detail was overlooked.

A while later, with the moon riding high in the heavens, among the foaming stars, they came out of the rocks, out into the smoothness of the north pasture. The herd was still there, bedded down quietly, with the men circling it on horseback, drooping a little in their saddles with the weariness that came at this hour of the morning when the whole world seemed to hover on the brink of sleep.

'We'll camp here for the night,' said Virginia quietly. As if to suit her words, she slid from the saddle and led her mount forward to the fire. Mark loosened the gun in his holster, then dropped beside her and walked forward.

The night air was cool and he was thankful to sit near the warmth of the fire and let it soak into his bones, soothing his tired back. Soon, he rolled the cup filled with steaming coffee between his hands and sat staring into the leaping flames.

The rest of the men were seated around the fire, stretching tired, weary limbs in front of them, chewing the food in their mouths, sipping the scalding coffee that had been brewed over the fire.

As he sat there Mark wondered where those outlaws and drovers were who had tried to kill them that evening, men led by the three outlaw brothers, who were determined now not only to kill him but to destroy Cal Ventner and the empire he had built out here. Probably they were still out there in the moon-thrown darkness of the plains, still riding, gathering together like a pack of coyotes, waiting and planning the moment when they would strike again – and the next time they would not turn and run, the next time would mean the end for one side or the other.

Minutes passed with no word from any of those who sat around the fire. The silence grew thick and heavy. Then Mark thrust a foot forward, kicked more wood on to the flames, and said to the girl seated beside him: 'You haven't told me yet how you managed to get me out of that jail, how you even knew I was there.'

'It wasn't difficult once I'd learned from the men here that you'd ridden into town to get some information about the Carsons, and to see the sheriff. I knew what had happened when my father went into Mason Bend and tried to get help from Sheriff Colman. I figured that if the same thing happened to you, you might find yourself in trouble. What happened in there – when they threw you into jail? A trumped-up charge? That's how Colman usually goes about his business.'

'He warned me to leave town, said he knew who I was and that there was a reward out for me dead or alive. He gave me the chance to ride out of town and keep on riding.' He knit his brows in puzzlement. 'I still don't know why he did that, unless he wanted to make sure that Carson knew I was there. Then, in the saloon, Hagberg, one of the men riding with the Carsons, tried to shoot me down. The rest was easy. Colman arrested me on a charge of murder, locked me in the jail, and while I was there the Carsons started stirring up the mob.'

'I thought it had to be something like that. Mort and I rode into town a little after midday and heard that you had been arrested.' Her smile was as easy as her manner as she went on: 'We picked up a mount just after dark, went into the jail while everyone else was in the saloon working themselves up before coming across to lynch you. The rest you know.'

He glanced at her in momentary surprise.

'So you stole that horse you brought for me?'

'Let's say that we borrowed it for the occasion,' broke in Kennedy. He uttered a loud, rumbling laugh. 'If Colman wants to hang us as horse thieves, he's welcome to ride out here and try.'

The flames ebbed in front of them and, in the near distance, the lowing of the cattle was stilled by sleep. The two men with the herd rode into camp and another two saddled up and rode out to take over watch. The camp rested.

Mark curled up in his blanket a couple of yards from the fire, watching the glowing embers through half-closed eyes. His body was weary but he could not sleep. There were too many thoughts running through his mind, chasing themselves around the corners of his brain.

It was a long while before he fell sleep, while the fire died slowly and the moon dropped smoothly down the vast shoulder of the heavens.

They rode into the ranch before midday with the sun beating down on them and the hills in the distance shimmering in the heat haze. Cal Ventner stood on the porch shading his eyes against the sun as they rode up, then he stepped down to meet them, eyeing Mark sharply. Then he switched his gaze to Virginia.

'Did you find him like I said?' he asked.

She nodded, slid from the saddle, stood beside her mount for a moment, her fair hair blowing about her face, glistening in the sunlight.

'Colman arrested him on a charge of murdering Clem Hagberg,' she said in an even voice. 'They were getting a lynch mob together to hang him.'

Ventner grinned mirthlessly. He glanced at Mark.

'Now you can see what kind of a sheriff we have in Mason Bend,' he averred. 'He's taken sides with those killers, and now we have the law against us.'

'Not the law,' Mark corrected him. 'Only the man who's supposed to uphold the law in these parts. There's quite a difference.'

'Well, maybe so. But I still don't see what we can do about it if he decides to swear in a posse and comes riding out here looking for you on a charge of murder.'

'You wouldn't let him come here and take Mark away, Father?' There was a note of astonishment in the girl's voice.

The other shook his head as he led the way into the house. 'I got no respect for the law now,' he said grimly.

'If'n they decided to come here, they'll get what they deserve. In the meantime, reckon you'd better get something to eat. I hear they tried for the herd that night and you fought them off.'

'That's right. No mistake about who was there.' Mark gave a brief nod. 'It was the Carsons all right. They tried to finish us last night, but the boys arrived in the nick of time.'

Ventner's eyebrows lifted. He looked at Mark from the other side of the room. 'What do you figure we ought to do now? Wait for them here? They'll bring plenty of men with them when they come.'

'I been thinking about that on the ride here.' Mark rubbed his chin. 'Seems we got to hit 'em before they're ready. I figure the best thing would be to take a group of the men into Mason Bend before they expect us. They'll be reckoning on us holing up here and that'll give them as much time as they need to get a gang of roughnecks together. They'll be able to choose their own time for attacking us.'

Ventner stared at him closely for a long moment, thinking things over in his mind. Finally he nodded.

'Take as many men as you think you'll need,' he said quietly.

'I'll go,' said Kennedy softly, his voice tight. 'After what happened last night, I reckon I got a score to settle with these outlaws, too.'

'I'll be glad to have you along,' Mark nodded. He remembered the coolness that the other had shown, knew that the foreman was a man who could be relied upon to keep his head if things got tough. 'We'll ride out after noon. We ought to reach Mason Bend by nightfall if we keep on riding. My guess is that they'll wait for a couple of days before they try anything more. They know that we're ready for 'em now and they'll want to try to take us by surprise.'

As he ate the food that was placed in front of him that noon, Mark felt the urgent restlessness bubbling up within him once more. There was the feeling that he was now very close to having his revenge on the men he had sought all these years, and the memory of it tightened his stomach muscles into a tight, hard knot. He ate mechanically, chewing his food slowly. There would not be long to wait now, he thought, if he had been right on his surmise about what the Carsons would do.

An hour later he roped a fresh horse from the corral and mounted up. There was a Winchester in the scabbard of the saddle and two Colts in his holsters.

The five men who were saddled up, waiting in the courtyard, were similarly armed.

The deep-seated weariness was still in his body and there were bruises on his chest and legs where that drover had tried to kill him the previous night. But the thought of meeting up with the Carson brothers in town drove all of that out of his mind, as he sat the saddle eagerly, feeling the hot touch of the sun on his shoulders and the sharp taste of dust in his mouth.

Before they rode out, Virginia Ventner came out and walked over to him, placing her hand on the bridle. There was a look of concern on her face as she looked up at him.

'Take care, Mark, won't you,' she said softly. 'They're dangerous men and they'll stop at nothing to kill you now that they know who you are and why you're hunting them. As far as they're concerned, you're more dangerous to them than my father.'

'I'll be careful, Virginia,' he promised. 'This is something I've got to get out of my system before I can even hope to be able to think straight again. When it's finished, maybe I'll be a whole man again, instead of only a part of one.'

She nodded wisely in silent understanding, held on to the bridle for a moment longer, then released it, stepping back.

'Watch for Sheriff Colman, too,' she warned. 'He's a coward at heart, but you've hurt his pride and manhood. He has to try to kill you now, or he'll never be able to live with himself. If he ever gets the chance, he'll shoot you in the back and think nothing of it.'

Mark looked at her for a moment with a penetrating attention. There was a quiet, speculative expression in her clear blue eyes, but he noticed the fine drawn lines around the edges of her mouth, knew that she was holding herself in tightly with an effort.

'Better warn your father to keep a sharp look out, too,' he said thinly. 'If they do decide to head this way while we're in town, you may have to hold them off until we can get back to help.'

'We'll be ready,' she promised. 'Maybe it might be best if we brought the main herd in from the north pasture, nearer the ranch. Then we would have four extra men to help.'

She went back to the porch, stood there shading her eyes from the glare of the sunlight as Mark wheeled his mount and rode out of the courtyard with the rest of the men behind him. The heat was a pressure on their bodies now, building up until it was barely bearable. Around them everything lay behind a trembling curtain as if they were viewing it through a thick layer of water.

CHAPTER 6

DARK DECISION

They rode their horses hard as they left the grassland behind, cutting across country to the north-east, heading for the trail into Mason Bend. As he rode, Mark Farrell watched the men who rode with him, glancing sideways out of his eyes at their faces, saw that they were in a quiet but inwardly savage mood. They had seen three of their companions shot down in cold blood by these vicious killers, knew that if things weren't taken into their own hands the same would happen to them. This had been building up for a long time, even before he had ridden into the ranch and asked for a job; but he knew that it had been his coming that had, in some strange way, brought things to a head as far as these men were concerned.

Previous to that they would not have considered trying to fight the sheriff and his men, and the outlaws who had ridden into town and taken it over. Now there was a change in them, something wrought more by his presence there than the reputation he had brought with him. They had seen for themselves that it was possible to stand up to these cold-blooded killers with a chance of winning through. There was no doubt in any of their minds that the odds were still against them, but they now faced up to that fact with a coolness that had been missing before.

He wondered how many times in the past these people had tried to get the sheriff to bring a posse together and ride out into the Badlands to the west after other outlaws, gun-slamming parasites who did their best to ruin the new territories before they were able to get on to their feet, only to find that the man who had taken over the post of sheriff had been in the pay of these outlaws.

A couple of miles further on they entered the rough country and were forced to slow their pace. In spite of the tight grip he had on himself, Mark found himself fretting inwardly at every second of the delay. But he knew it would be foolish to try to push their mounts in this rough terrain. One slip, one foot set wrong, and it would mean a lame horse, and they would then never reach the town before nightfall.

Kennedy rode alongside him, eyes scanning the horizons, alert for trouble, although not expecting it out here. Any trouble they were likely to meet would be in town. He swung his gaze abruptly to Mark, gave him a tight sort of grin.

'Must say I never figured I'd be riding out with a man like you, heading into big trouble like this, when I signed on for Mister Ventner.' He threw a dark glance over the rest of the men. 'Wonder how many of them will really fight when it comes to the point.'

'So long as they stand their ground, we ought to make out fine,' Mark said.

He pursed his lips, threw a swift glance at the sun, estimated how long they had already been on the trail. Their dust stretched away behind them into the rocks, marking their position, he knew, to anyone who might be up there watching for riders along this part of the trail.

Kennedy lifted his gaze. 'Looks like we're in for a storm,' he said quietly, inclining his head towards the ominous purple bar of cloud that lay low on the horizon directly ahead of them. Even from that distance it was possible to see that it was moving swiftly towards them, hazing details, driving down on them.

But this was no storm of rain and lightning such as had struck them last night. Mark realised that instantly. That ominous grey-purple cloud meant only one thing, a dust storm, a roaring wind that whipped the alkali dust from the face of the desert and carried it high into the air, hurling it over the wide prairie with an incredible swiftness. There was no chance to turn their horses and try to run before it, even if they had wanted to.

Within minutes the wind rose, blowing straight in their faces off the Badlands, plucking at their tunics and leggings, swirling about them, shrieking in their ears. In a way, reflected Mark, before the full fury of the storm reached them, it might help riding through it like this, even if it did mean their progress would be slowed even further. Bart Carson would never expect anyone to ride through it and would not be ready for them when they rode into Mason Bend. It would also prevent any lookouts on the outskirts of town from spotting them before dark.

He lowered his head as the dark, ominous cloud swept down on them, driving in on a wide front. The full fury of the dust storm hit them a few moments later, the sunlight was blotted out entirely, and only a strangely pale glow filtered about them. The wind whipped the stinging grains of sand – millions upon untold millions of them – into their faces, blinding them, cutting into their flesh, working its way into their clothing; a swirling, yellow blanket, a tumult of sound.

He tried to breathe normally, but even with the

bandana over his face it was impossible. There was the feel of heat all about them even though the direct sunlight had been dimmed by the storm. Their ears hurt from the thin, high-pitched wail of the shrieking wind.

For long weary minutes that stretched themselves out into painful eternities, they rode with their eyes tightly closed, allowing the horses to pick their own way forward, knowing that it would be not only foolish but suicidal to try to hurry them now. The storm would blow itself out in its own good time and, until it did, they would be riding blind, relying on the hidden instinct of their mounts to keep them on the narrow trail.

After an hour of riding through that shrieking tumult, Mark would not have been overly surprised if half of the men had decided to turn back and retrace their steps to the ranch. But they stuck with him, cursing a little under their breath, heads pulled right down, their faces totally hidden by the bandanas.

The horses, too, suffered from the fury of the storm. Out here, on the very edge of the Badlands, it had been known for such a storm to drive horses crazy, to send them running out into the desert, whipping them into a tempestuous fury which was impossible for the rider to control

Inwardly, he guessed that in the past a few trail bosses may have tried to bring their cattle through to the railroad across this country, may have attempted to seek a shorter trail than that which headed north and then east, but even they, iron-willed as they may have been, would have been forced to yield to this tremendous force of Nature.

There was no doubt that these were the crazy lands where a man would have to fight to survive. As they walked their horses along the narrow trail, heading east, the wind died a little. They were climbing into the hills now and the sand and wind lay below them so that they were only catching the upper fringe of the storm. There was still sufficient force in the wind, battering at their bruised and bleeding faces, to force them to ride low in the saddle, bodies bunched forward over the pommel.

But now there were no longer those itching, irritating grains of sand that battered them from all sides at the lower level. Mark lifted his head and drew in a rasping breath. His mouth seemed to be lined with sand, and his eyes, even though he had kept them tightly closed for most of the time, were smarting and tender.

Blinking, he stared ahead of him, kicking spurs to the horse's flanks. The sorrel bounded forward, tossing its head. It still wanted three hours or so to sundown, but they still had plenty of miles to cover in that time. They crossed a hump-backed bridge, rode swiftly down the far side. Here the wind died abruptly, as if someone had shut off a tap, and they were able to see clearly again. It was as well that they could. In places here the trail was so narrow that they were forced to ride in single file, and one wrong step could have meant that horse and rider plunged to their deaths over a forty-foot drop on the edge of the trail.

There was little said on that long ride to Mason Bend. The men were all engrossed with their own thoughts, which they preferred to keep private. Hard-faced and stony-eyed, their nostrils pinched and white after the lashing of the storm, their minds were too full for any conversation as they contemplated what might lie ahead for them.

Mark saw that some were fingering their rifles absently, while others sat tall and straight now in the saddle, easing the agony of cramped muscles in their backs, staring straight ahead into the distance, eyes searching out the black smudge on the horizon which would indicate the position of the town.

Once they reached the end of the mountain trail, came down out of the hills and joined the main trail from Mason Bend to the west, they did not spare their horses, but pushed them to the limit. More and more, Mark felt the tight tenseness growing in him. It manifested itself in the taut expression on his face, the way he kept touching the butts of the Colts in their well-worn holsters, and the compressed set of his lips.

Darkness was touching the eastern heavens when they came within sight of the town. Mark reined his mount while they were still half a mile away, holding up his hand as the others reached him.

'If the Carsons are here, they'll either be holed up in the hotel or with the sheriff,' he said. 'Keep your eyes open and be ready to use your guns. They might be waiting for us, but I doubt it.'

The men nodded, hitched their gunbelts higher about their waists, then rode up on either side of him. In a loose bunch they moved forward into the waiting town.

The township of Mason Bend had been born many years before. It had not been planned. There had been few folk around in those days, and nobody there to formulate any plans for its construction. It had been on the edge of the Indian territory in those days, when the river, born in the hills, came tumbling down along the perimeter of the Badlands and close to the sweet, succulent grasslands which now formed the ranches where the beef cattle were raised.

Mason Bend had been built by the guts and sweat, the hardships and tears of the men and women who had been blessed with the vision and foresight that had seen there would some day be a big town there, a place on the map. Lumber had been brought in, nails and hammers. A store had been thrown up on one side of the wide, hard-beaten trail, and then a couple of saloons. There had been prospectors out there in the hills, panning the streams for gold, working the mines, cutting their way into the hard rocks in search of the precious yellow metal that would mean wealth for them for the rest of their lives.

But it had been for men such as these that the saloons and gambling joints had been erected on either side of the track. For with the builders had come the gamblers, the cardsharps, the killers. They had taken most of the gold, had brought in the cheap whiskey and the girls, with their bright eyes and painted faces.

Gradually the frontier had been pushed westward. The covered wagons had come through, carrying their cargoes of men and women and children, heading west for the new and promised land, opening up the country.

But not all of them had passed through. There had been some who had paused here, liked what they had seen and turned aside. The town had grown, more shacks and houses were built, and it had gradually taken shape. The citizens had tried to bring law and order there, had elected men to keep the law for them, honest and fearless men who had worn the star of sheriff and fought the outlaws.

Without the gamblers, the cardsharps, the profiteers, the town would never have been built. That was an established and undisputed fact. But the time had come when these men and their ways had to move aside for something better, something more stable and secure. There had been mistakes in the beginning, of course, hundreds of mistakes. But these people had set out to build themselves a town out of the open wilderness and, by God, they had got the job done.

Now it lay there in the quiet dusk, dark and shadowed. Violence had come back to Mason Bend, a return to the old lawless days. Soon, if something was not done about it, they would remain there, and it would have been better if the men and women who had built the place had simply kept on riding west....

Mark ran a dry tongue over equally dry lips as they entered

the wide street. He rubbed the dust and sand from his eyes and drew a deep breath into his lungs. A hand dropped to the heavy belt around his middle and, almost of their own volition, his fingers loosened the gun in the holster, half lifted it out, then dropped it back again. There were a few horses in the street, lights shining yellowly from the windows of the saloons and stores.

He lifted his eyes, glanced instinctively in the direction of the hotel on the corner. There were no horses tethered to the hitching rail outside. Pursing his lips, he let his gaze wander as he rode slowly forward.

The dark shadows of the men on the quiet boardwalks watched as the group of men rode into town, but made no move. A woman came out on to the veranda overlooking the saloon nearby, glanced down at them, then went back quickly inside.

The slow rhythmic tread of the horses' hoofs seemed to be the only sound in the town. One step after another, they rode up into Mason Bend until they were level with the hotel. Pausing for a moment, Mark eyed the empty hitching rail, then swung his glance swiftly in the direction of the sheriff's office. There was a solitary stud tied to the post outside. He recognised Colman's mount instantly, nodded towards it and turned his mount.

Tension crackled in the street of the town as they reined in, in front of the office. In the dimness Mark was able to see the light inside and Sheriff Colman seated behind his desk. Deliberately he leaned forward over the pommel and called:

'Colman! I want a word with you – outside!'

Through the glass he saw the other's body stiffen, abruptly, knew that the sheriff had recognised his voice. Instinctively the man hurled his body down on to the floor behind the desk, knocking the lamp off with a wide sweep of his right arm as he went down. The light went out and the room was in darkness, but not for long. A couple of seconds later Mark saw the swift stabs of flame as Colman opened fire from his hiding place at the back of the desk, and the window shattered into a hundred fragments as the bullets slammed through it. He ducked swiftly, heard the vicious hum of the slug as it tore through the air close to his head. Then he was out of the saddle, moving forward, swiftly and cat-like, the Colts in his hands, motioning the rest of the men back.

Kicking open the door, he fired off a couple of shots, Then darted inside, hurling himself to one side as the sheriff fired madly at him. The bullets crashed into the woodwork of the door, splintering the upright.

Acting on instinct, he slitted his eyes against the flash of the other's weapons, then fired. The shots made a hard metallic rattle in the room. He was not baffled by the stabbing explosions of the sheriff's Colts, nor the hot stench of powder in his nostrils. He knew the other was still there, crouched behind the desk, probably shaking like a leaf, his mind whirling as he tried to think of a way out.

Gripping his guns hard, he stared into the smoke, blinking his eyes to adjust them to the darkness. He could make out the harsh sound of the other's breathing a few feet away.

'I don't want to have to kill you, Colman, but if you don't toss out those guns and move out where I can see you, with your hands held high, that's just what I'm going to do. The choice is yours.'

As he spoke he rolled to one side and the slug which had been fired in the direction of his voice passed a couple of feet from him as he lay under the smashed window.

'You don't think I'd take the word of a self-confessed killer, do you?' Colman's voice was harsh and rapid in the darkness. He seemed to be trying to buck up his failing courage. 'You just want to shoot me down in cold blood, along with the rest of those killers you've brung into town with you.'

A bullet thunked into the wood near his head. He flinched, but kept quite still, knowing that the other's nerve was going to crack real soon.

The silence in the room lengthened. Outside he could hear the horses milling around.

The sheriff's rasping breaths were oddly loud in the silence and he must have suddenly realised that they could give him away, for they ceased for a moment, then he exhaled hoarsely, letting his air go in a sudden rush.

'You still there, Farrell?' he croaked.

'That's right, Sheriff.' Deliberately, Mark laid stress on the last word. 'All you've to do is throw out your guns and get on your feet.'

'Just why are you wanting to kill me?' There was a plaintive note in the other's high-pitched tone now. 'I only did what I had to do when I arrested you. You can't hold it against a man for doing his duty.'

'Was it your duty to throw in your lot with those Carson brothers? Was it your duty to sit back and do nothing when it was reported to you that cattle were being rustled and men shot down from ambush on the prairie?'

'Well – I had to have proof. And as for the Carsons, I ain't having anything to do with them now. They're killers, all right. You were right the first time and once I get a posse together, we're going to ride out and hunt them down. I was just on the point of getting men together when you turned up, and if you'd like to come with us, we could—'

'You're talking too much,' Mark broke in as the other's flow of words went on and on. 'I reckon that you're stallin' for time, hoping that the Carsons will get back into town. I'm going to count up to three, and if you haven't tossed out your guns by that time, I'm going to kill you. Understand?'

He heard the faint slithering sound as he shifted his own position slightly.

'One . . .'

'Now, hold on a minute, Farrell. I still don't trust you and—'

'Two . . .'

He heard the sharp click of a hammer falling on an empty chamber as the other got swiftly to his feet, a dark shadow behind the desk, trying to shoot him down from there. Mark started up, then staggered back as he saw the other's arm swing forward, tossing the empty gun. It struck him high on the chest, knocking him back against the wall. Before he could bring up either of his guns, line them up on the other's body, the sheriff, with a courage born of desperation, hurled himself across the room, arms outstretched, fingers clawed as they reached for Mark's eyes.

Mark was getting to his feet as the other's body hit him solidly. He went down again, half stunned by the heavy metal of the gun which the other had thrown at him.

Savagely, instinctively, he lashed out with his right hand, bunching it into a fist. It caught the other on the side of the head as he came boring in, kneeing Mark in the pit of the stomach. Gasping a little as pain lanced through his body, Mark braced himself, kicked with his feet, wriggling from under the other's heavy body, heaving him aside as he clawed his way to his feet.

The sheriff was a beefy man, but had allowed himself to go to fat and he was out of condition, puffing and gasping through his open mouth as he fought for his life, twisting, surging against Mark with an almost superhuman strength.

Mark came upright, stood for a moment, leaning against the wall at his back, fighting to maintain his balance. There was a blackness in front of his eyes as his consciousness threatened to leave him and every breath that he sucked down into his heaving lungs sent a stab of red-edged agony through his chest, lancing into his muscles.

All the time that they had fought, the other had not uttered a single sound, not one solitary cry for help. Colman staggered upright. Almost too late, Mark saw that his right hand was no longer empty. He had picked up one of Mark's own guns that he had been forced to drop when the other had attacked him so unexpectedly. There was no time to think. Already the barrel of the Colt was lifting, lining itself up on his chest. He moved in, his right hand flashing for the other's arm, fingers gripping tightly around the sheriff's wrist, squeezing hard, forcing the gun downward so that it was impossible for the other to angle it for a killing shot.

Savagely, grunting through clenched teeth, he forced the other's wrist back until Colman had to drop the gun before his wrist snapped.

Swiftly, teeth drawn back in an animal-like grin, the other reared up, hurled Mark away from him so that he struck the side of the heavy desk with the small of his back. Colman came in, breathing harshly. He staggered forward, swaying a little from side to side, arms held low as if to wrap them around Mark's body and crush the life out of him. Lashing out with his left foot, Mark caught the other hard on the shin, heard his sudden bleat of surprise and agony, and followed up the blow with a hammering right cross to the jaw.

Colman toppled forward and Mark finished it all with a vicious downward chop to the back of the other's neck, catching him just behind the ear. The lawman went down as if pole-axed and lay unmoving on the floor. Breathing heavily, Mark went over to the door, opened it and called:

'Better come in here, Mort. Sheriff's out cold, and he's probably the only one who can tell us where the others are.'

Kennedy slid smoothly from the saddle, threw Mark a swift glance as he noticed the blood on the side of his face, the drawn expression on his tight lips, then stepped past him and bent over the unconscious figure of the sheriff. A moment late he had grasped the man by the shoulders, heaved him upright so that his inert body stood on tiptoe, and slung him unceremoniously over his shoulder, carrying him outside, where he lowered him into the dust in the middle of the street.

'Any sign of the Carsons while I was in there?' Mark asked.

Kennedy glanced up, shook his head in answer.

'The town's been quiet,' said one of the other men. He stared idly at the sheriff. 'What you going to do with him? Take him back with us?'

'Maybe. But we've got to bring him round and get some information out of him right now. If the Carsons ain't in town, I want to know where they are and when they rode out. He's the only one likely to know.'

'If he does, he'll soon tell us, I promise you that,' muttered Kennedy. 'I reckon that he knows he's finished now. He won't want to take the rap for the others.'

He walked across the street to the horse trough, brought back some water in the sheriff's own hat and flung it over the unconscious man's face. Colman stirred, spluttered and coughed for a moment, then sat up, staring about him, looking into the grim faces of the men who surrounded him. A look of fear crossed his face as his gaze flashed back to Mark.

'You going to shoot me here and now?' he said, his voice pitched a little higher than normal. 'That would be murder.'

'No more than when you held me in jail, waiting for that mob to come along and take me out to string up from the nearest convenient tree,' Mark told him grimly. 'But at the moment, we want some information. It depends on whether or not we get it, and whether you tell the truth, if we kill you or not.'

'I don't know anything, I swear it.'

Mark shook his head slowly. A thin smile spread over his face, but there was no mirth in it, and the other man must have seen the promise of death in the clear grey eyes that watched him pitilessly for he blanched, licked his lips slowly.

'You're going to tell us where the Carsons are right now,' Mark said softly.

'I don't know. They're over at the hotel.' The lawman's gaze slid past Mark in the direction of the tall brick building on the edge of the square.

'Try again, Sheriff.' Mark thinned his lips. 'You know damned well that they rode out of town with some other men during the afternoon. Where did they go and what do they intend to do?'

'I don't know, I tell you.' A muscle twitched uncontrollably high in the other's cheek as he lay there, propping himself up on his arms, looking from one man to the next. His features were stiff and he seemed to have difficulty in swallowing.

'There are one or two tricks I learned from the Indians,' said Kennedy softly and deliberately, moving forward. The sheriff squeaked and tried to get to his feet. 'I reckon I could use 'em on him and he'd tell us soon enough. He doesn't look the kind of *hombre* to me who'd stand a lot of torture.'

His words had the desired effect, as Mark had anticipated that they would. Colman put up his right arm as if to fend off the others, mouth working, but with no sound coming out. Then he blurted: 'They'll kill me if they find out that I've told you anything.'

'And we'll kill you if you don't,' Mark said grimly. 'You can take your choice, Colman. Only remember – we're here now, the Carsons ain't – and if we catch up with them in time, they won't be coming back. But you'll live to stand your trial.'

He took a step forward, bent and grasped the other by
the front of the shirt, hauling him to his feet, where he
stood swaying, a little trickle of saliva running down his
chin.

'If there's anything in this world that I hate, it's a
double-dealing sheriff, a crooked lawman. I reckon we
ought to try you and hang you here and now, but you may
be of some use to us in the future. Now speak your piece
and it had better be the truth.'

'They've been rounding up as many men as they can to
ride with them, mostly some of the drovers and gamblers,
promising them plenty once they take the Ventner ranch.'

'You sure they rode out to the Ventner ranch? All of
them?'

'That's right. I heard 'em talking in the saloon.' The
other was speaking rapidly now, the words spilling from
him. Mark did not doubt that he was speaking the truth,
but this was something he had dreaded hearing. It meant
that, unwittingly perhaps, the Carsons had been too
smart for them. While they had been riding into town,
taking care of the sheriff, the others had been moving
out to attack the ranch. They had split their force now
that he had brought these men out here on what was
virtually a wild goose chase. He doubted if they would be
able to get back to the ranch in time, but it was the only
course open to them, if they were to save Ventner and
Virginia.

He stepped back from the sheriff. There was nothing to
fear from the other now. He was a broken, shattered man.
His manhood was gone and his pride with it. He had
played for big stakes and the indications at the moment
were that he had lost. If the Carsons won through, then
they would take care of Sheriff Colman themselves, in
their own way. If a miracle happened, and the Carsons and
everything they stood for were wiped out of the State of
Kansas, then the ordinary people of Mason Bend would

know how to deal with a crooked lawman. Either way, Sheriff Colman was finished, and he knew it.

'What do we do with him?' asked Kennedy, as Mark moved quickly forward and swung himself up into the saddle. 'Take him with us?'

'No. Leave him here. He's finished. Somehow I don't think it will be too healthy for him around town once the folk here get to know the kind of man he really is, who his friends are.'

Sheriff Colman stood swaying, one hand against the wall of the office, eyeing them through blurred eyes as Mort Kennedy climbed into the saddle, wheeled his horse away from the hitching post. A beaten, defeated man, no longer safe in the town he had tried to run.

'You're a lot of goddarned fools if you reckon you can stand up to the Carsons,' he said through bruised and swollen lips. 'They've got too many men riding with them. Long before you can get back to the ranch, they'll have overrun it and shot down everyone inside. They swore they'd do that and then they'll come back for you, Farrell. I only hope that I'm around when that happens. I still want the pleasure of seeing you dangling from the end of a rope.'

'Somehow,' said Mark grimly, 'I have the feeling that end is reserved for you.' He jerked his mount's head around sharply, called to the rest of the men and headed out of town, setting his horse at a gallop, their hoofs drumming on the hard surface of the street.

Cal Ventner stood by the window of the ranch, looking out over the wide stretch of the courtyard and the corral that lay beyond. The air outside was motionless now that the evening was drawing in and the sun was getting ready to drop down out of sight behind the tall mountains on the skyline, falling into blackness like a round penny going into a box. It was something he had seen so often during the years that he had been there, that it was a wonder he had never got used to it. But these were the most magnificent sunsets it was possible to see anywhere in the whole wide world, he felt sure of that.

Back east, through the smoke and haze of the big cities, one never saw colours like these, reds and greens and golds, all splashed across the sky with the wonder and brilliance of a painter's brush. He drew in a deep breath, rubbed his chin with the palm of his hand. In the kitchen he heard Virginia moving around as she stacked the dishes away.

When her mother had died he had thought it impossible to carry on here, living with the memories of her, and with a girl child to raise. But somehow he had managed and now he had built up this ranch into one of the biggest and finest in the whole state. Yet he would lose it, would have it snatched from him as sure as anything if Mark Farrell didn't succeed in stopping those three gunslammers who had vowed to take it away from him and kill him into the bargain.

It had been a cruel trick of Fate when she had decreed that he was to be the man who had to testify against those men, and an even crueller one when they had been jailed rather than hanged as they had deserved. But the really punishing blow had come when they had busted out of jail and finally succeeded in trailing him here.

He felt the fear ride him again, felt the tightening of his stomach muscles as he stared out over the valley, where the grass shone with a warm, blue glow now that the sun was almost gone. In the west the blues were deepening and the red was almost gone. Another world was taking shape and form right there in front of his eyes, changing even as he stood and watched it. A colder world of blues and purples, with lengthening shadows that stretched out so swiftly across the courtyard that he imagined he could almost see them growing.

It was now more than nine hours since Farrell had ridden out with those five men, heading for town. He had doubted the wisdom of taking so few men, but as Farrell had rightly pointed out, there was just the chance that Bart Carson might be too clever for them, might already have sent his men out to the ranch, and it would be sheer suicide to leave it totally undefended.

As it was, there were five men inside the building, apart from himself, and another four near the corral, the men who had brought the herd down from the north meadow late that afternoon.

Whether there would be enough of them to stop a large force of men he did not know.

Virginia came into the room, saw him standing by the window, and walked over to him, her eyes dark with speculation.

'You're worried, aren't you, Father? Is it because of me?'

He turned, took her outstretched hands in his, paused for a moment before nodding his head slowly.

'In a way – yes. I wish you had gone back east while all of this trouble was brewing. I suppose it was my fault, in a way, for not realising that trouble like this was coming.'

She smiled, and there was no fear in her face.

'I'm not afraid of these men, Father.' She pulled her hands away, went over to one of the chairs and sat down in it, looking out through the window at the darkening world outside. 'I know that you've often been disappointed because I wasn't a boy, someone you could really leave all of this to and know that it would remain in the family. But everything that I've ever known and loved is here. Do you think I would want to go away and leave it when danger threatens it – and you?'

'I know you wouldn't.' He went over and sat beside her, one arm around her shoulders. 'But if danger does come, then we'll be ready to meet it.'

She looked up at him. 'You think those men may ride out here before Mark gets back?'

'They may. We'd be foolish to ignore that possibility.' He bit his lower lip, then got to his feet again and went back to the window, staring out along the trail that ran over the low hill before vanishing in mystery down the other side.

'I wish I knew what was happening in Mason Bend. I've got the feeling in my bones that there's something wrong, that we've overlooked something really important.'

Virginia did not answer, but leaned back in the chair, keeping her eyes on him. In the corral a horse danced skittishly for a few moments, then settled down once more. The herd was bedded down on the slope of the hill in the near distance and Ventner could just make out the shapes of the four men on horseback, circling it slowly. If anyone did try to sneak upon the ranch from that direction, they would be the first to know about it and would raise the alarm.

The first stars were showing in the clear heavens now that the sun had gone. There were no clouds and the moon, not yet risen, would come up around midnight, giving them plenty of light to see by, if needed.

How long he stood there he did not really know. Now that the sun was down, time seemed to have little meaning. The stars overhead did not seem to move across the sky in the same noticeable way, giving some indication of the passage of time.

It grew darker and colder. Outside a couple of the men moved in from the corral, walked on to the porch, their booted heels sounding louder on the wooden slats. Then they pushed open the door and came inside.

Cal heard them talking together in low voices, so soft that it was impossible for him to pick out the words. Maybe they were just about as scared as he was, he figured, wondering what the coming night was going to bring in the way of trouble.

The outer door closed. For a long moment there was silence over everything. It was so quiet that he could hear his own heart thumping in his chest, felt sure that Virginia must also hear it and know how scared he was.

Then there was no time to think about that, no time to wonder what they should do when the time for action came, for, at that precise moment, the first shot rang out, cutting through the stillness of the night.

CHAPTER 7

DEATH AT NIGHT

More shots blasted through the stillness around the ranch, and for perhaps five seconds Cal Ventner stood at the window, feeling isolated, scarcely able to take in what those sounds meant. Then he was leaping back into the room, away from the window where he was silhouetted against the light of the paraffin lamp on the table, yelling for the men in the other room.

Dropping full length on the floor behind the window, he heard the savage splintering of wood close over his head, the vicious smack of the slugs as they tore through the glass, shattering it into fragments, hammering into the wall at his back. He had a sudden creepy feeling about it all, and a small roll of panic in the pit of his stomach caused him to shift sideways, jerking his feet convulsively. Then he caught himself abruptly, saw that Virginia had already moved swiftly to the side of the window, grabbing the long-barrelled Winchester.

Bart Carson and his men had travelled fast and with great secrecy, for somehow they had managed to get within shooting distance of the ranch house without being spotted by his men. He had prided himself on his scout system, but it was obvious now that it had let him down – and badly.

Drawing the Colt from its holster, he lifted himself gently and cautiously from the floor where he had thrown himself, careful not to lift his head above the level of the window-ledge. More bullets were striking the side of the house.

Two of the men came barging into the room, stood hesitant for a moment, then ran back as he yelled at them to take up their positions in the other rooms. Even as they left he heard the firing swing round, knew that the Carsons had brought plenty of men with them, possibly every man they had been able to find in Mason Bend willing to ride with them, and they had already virtually surrounded the house, were firing from all sides.

He heard men yell outside and, above the sound of gunfire, there was the rumble of hoofs in the corral, then out in the dark courtyard as someone opened the gates and let their horses loose, stampeding them into the hills in the distance.

Evidently Carson was taking no chances, intended to make certain that no one left there to fetch help. The savage destruction of the gunfire continued for several seconds, unabated, a storm of lead that flailed against the walls of the house, hammered through the smashed glass of the windows and hummed across the room.

He pressed himself flat against the wall on one side of the window. Nothing in the whole of his imagination was anything like this. He tried to guess how many men were out there, weighing their own chances of fighting them off until Farrell discovered in Mason Bend what had happened and came hightailing it back, bringing the other men with him. A little voice at the back of his mind warned him that even if they pushed their tired horses to the utmost limit, it would be dawn before they could reach them.

Every muscle in his body was stretched so tight that he began to ache all over. The muscles of his legs were drawn into a cramp, but his mind was still very clear and sharp. He followed the shifting fire from outside quite easily. There were moments when it was smashing against the rear of the building, answered by the fire of his own men in the rooms back there watching every direction of attack, then it would suddenly switch and swing back to the front.

'Can you see them, Father?' Virginia's voice reached him from the other side of the room.

He edged forward a few inches, tried to peer through the window. The paraffin lamp had been smashed to smithereens by the first burst of gunfire and the room was now in total darkness. Outside there was a faint residual glow in the sky and, by the light, he could just make out a dark shadow that slipped forward from the direction of the corral.

Possibly the man who had let the horses loose, he thought grimly. Swiftly, he jerked up the Colt, sighted and fired in the same moment, saw the man suddenly pause as if listening, then stagger, hands clutching at his belly. He weaved forward a couple of paces, then collapsed on his face in the dust near the water trough.

'They're all around the house, daughter,' he said, urgently. 'We'll have to hold them all off through the night, otherwise we're finished. They'll probably try to rush us soon. If they think that Farrell and the others are in here with us, they may hold off for a little while rather than risk running into their fire, but once they figure that he isn't here, they'll force home their attack in the hope of overrunning us before we get help.'

He fired a couple of shots at another figure that broke cover and ran, hunched over, across the far side of the courtyard, but both bullets missed, kicking up dust around the man's feet, sending him diving for cover. The return blast of fire was almost immediate, and he was forced to pull back his head as slugs hummed dangerously close.

'One dead,' he said harshly, 'but God knows how many more there are out there.'

As if in answer to that, a voice yelled loudly from somewhere in the darkness.

''You're finished, Ventner. Why don't you give up and come on out with your hands lifted? The same goes for those men with you. I got no quarrel with your hands. If they come out now, they'll go free – I promise you that.'

'You think we'd take the promise of a cold-blooded murderer like you, Carson?' It was Virginia who called out the words in a clear, loud tone.

Although her father did not know it at the time, it was that, more than anything else, which stopped any of the other men in the ranch house from taking Bart Carson at his word and walking out of that building with their hands over their heads. Had there been any of them ready to do that, ready to surrender on the chance that their lives would be spared, that clear, calm voice shamed them out of such thoughts.

'All right, we've got all night,' Carson called. 'You won't be able to hold out much longer. You don't have all that much ammunition. And there ain't no way you can get out of that place without being shot down by my men.'

Cal heard some of the outlaws running fast and clumsy near the barn. He heard voices, sharp-calling in the near distance. The firing died down for a spell and the silence settled over everything again.

He tried to figure out what the others were doing out there in the darkness. There seemed little doubt that some kind of plan was being built up against them, but what it was he could not imagine. The shouting went on for several minutes, and it reminded him of nothing more than a wolf-pack.

A sudden movement at the edge of his vision brought his head snapping round. A man ran out of the darkness some yards away, rushing in the direction of the barn. He snapped a couple of shots at the running figure, saw him stagger as a bullet took the man in the leg, then he limped forward, bobbing and weaving from side to side so that the second bullet went wide. A moment later he was gone around the side of the house.

Back in Cal's head was the knowledge that he had been taken by surprise by this attack, badly caught off guard. They were holed up in this place, unable to move and unless Farrell and the other men reached them soon, they were surely finished.

Seconds later more shots blasted against the wall of the house, there was the tinkle of shattered glass; then a moment later the door of the room burst open and one of the other hands rushed in.

'They've fired the barn!' he called harshly. 'If the wind carries the flames this way, they'll be able to smoke us out.'

The moon, round and yellow, came up an hour before midnight and seemed to hug the eastern horizon for a long while before climbing slowly and with reluctance into the night sky. It shone with a pale, cold light on the band of men who rode their tired mounts hell for leather across the open stretch of ground, down into rocky ravines where the clear trickle of water showed bright in the moonlight, out on to narrow, winding trails that twisted and wound around the side of the hills, the hoofs of their horses kicking stones over the edge of the sheer drop on one side, stones that rattled down for nearly a hundred feet before they came to rest at the bottom. If the men who rode so swiftly thought of the danger that could come from one false move of their mounts, they gave no outward sign.

In the lead, Mark Farrell raked spurs along the flanks of his mount, felt it respond gallantly, although it had carried him for several miles already with scarcely any rest. He knew that they ought to rest up and give their horses a chance to blow, but at the back of his mind there was the knowledge that every second might be important now, that they had to reach the ranch as quickly as possible.

In his mind's eye he could visualise what was happening there at that moment. Carson would lose no time in attacking the defenders inside the ranch house. He evidently had the men with him to overwhelm them and he doubted if Ventner and the men with him would be able to hold out throughout the whole of the night.

A mile further on and they entered the timber, and here progress was slow. The horses could make little speed on the soft floor of pine needles which had fallen and settled there over half a century. The timber was first growth pine, thick and huge at the base but tapering up into the long trunk that rose slenderly into the heavens. They were out of the moonlight here and riding in almost total darkness with only their inborn senses to guide them. Mark pulled deep lungfuls of the sweet-smelling air down into his lungs and tried to tell himself that they would make it to the ranch in time, promising himself inwardly that if they didn't he would not rest until every single man in that outlaw band, drover or otherwise, had been hunted down and destroyed.

He knew that the killers had a ten-mile lead on them at the very least, and if they had ridden hard and fast could possibly have reached the ranch a little after sundown.

They were still in the timber when, lifting his head, he heard the single, distance-starved echo. A gunshot that shattered the stillness of the night. He listened intently for any repetition, but there was none. The night was still again, giving nothing away.

They held to the rim of the ridges as far as possible, where there was a little moonlight filtering through the branches of the trees overhead, giving them light by which to ride more swiftly. The red-barked trees fled swiftly by them, vanished into the overall darkness of the timber at their backs, and still they had not come out on to the plain which led through the rocks to the north pasture. The sense of urgency that had been riding him fiercely ever since they had left Mason Bend was still in him, growing stronger and more insistent with every minute that passed.

They dropped into narrow ravines, crossed one rise after another, always bearing south, down from the hills. The men riding with him, their faces mainly in shadow, looked neither to their right or left. It was as if they all knew with a strange certainty that the only damage which lay in store for them lay directly ahead, at the ranch, that there would be no attacks on them out here, no more ambushes, no more shooting from cover. The showdown had come and they were riding swiftly to meet it.

The moon lifted clear of the horizon, grew more brilliant. It was a cold light that it threw over everything, highlighting the narrow crevasses, spotlighting the ridges around them. They rode with short switchback courses, now dipping down all of the time, lower and lower as midnight came and went.

There was, thought Mark impatiently, undoubtedly a better and safer way of moving off this ridge of ground, but it would have taken them another hour to have negotiated it and time was at a high premium that night. It took them close on two hours to clear the ridges, to ride out on to the plains.

The horses were winded now, but still they continued to push them, men who had passed beyond weariness or exhaustion, men who had only one thought in their minds, the urge to kill, led by Mark Farrell, wanted gunman in half a dozen states, a man filled with burning hatred, a tight anger that filled his mind to the exclusion of everything else.

The north pasture, when they reached it, was empty of cattle, except for small bunches of steers, missed during the hurried round-up. The men rode by them without a sideways glance.

Minutes passed and lengthened into an hour. The thunder of their horses' hoofs was the only sound that disturbed the long stillness of the prairie. By the time they reached the low rise that overshadowed the ranch, dawn was just an hour away and it was still sufficiently dark, even in the moonlight, for them to see the red glow that flickered and burned in the direction of the ranch.

'My God, they've fired the barn!' yelled one of the men. He leaned forward in the saddle, pointing.

Mark narrowed his eyes, stared grimly at the scene before them. He could not hear any shooting, and a stab of fear touched his heart at the realisation that they were too late, that Carson, his brothers and the men they had brought with them, had already completed their foul deed and had ridden off after setting fire to the barn. But there was no point in taking unnecessary chances. The killers might still be there and they had no way of knowing how many of them there were.

'Better dismount and we'll move in from behind,' he ordered. 'Bring your rifles.'

The men slid wearily from the saddle, flexed their limbs to ease them of the cramp brought on by the long hours of riding, then followed Mark down the hillside, past the still sleeping herd, in the direction of the ranch. They were less than two hundred yards away, near the bushes that grew along the edge of the narrow stream at the foot of the hill, when the firing started up again, the sharp, barking echoes ringing on the still air.

Swiftly Mark motioned the men to spread out. They went down instantly, keeping out of sight. Return fire was coming from the windows of the ranch, the tulipping flames from the muzzles of the guns clearly visible in the darkness.

Mark heaved a sigh of relief. So they were not all dead

inside the ranch. He slithered forward. Already a plan was beginning to form in his mind as he lifted his head cautiously to try to determine the positions of the outlaws and how many there were. Certainly he did not think they would be expecting an attack from the rear. Carson, if he had already guessed that some of the men had ridden into town, would not be expecting them to get back before dawn. He might be a little careless about watching his rear, and that was exactly what Mark wanted.

To ride down there with guns blazing, hoping to take the others by surprise and smash the ring of steel that Carson had forged around the ranch house would be the worst thing he could do. They would have to run the gauntlet not only of Carson's men but of the fire coming from inside the ranch.

He cast about him for some means of utilising the element of surprise, was still searching when there was a faint rustle in the bushes beside him, and Kennedy came wriggling forward. He caught hold of Mark's arm and pointed to the right.

Glancing round, Mark noticed, half hidden among the bushes, the tall wagon, piled high with hay and straw, standing at the top of the slope.

A swiftly appraising glance told him what was in the other's mind. Once sent down that slope, its path would take that wagon through the densest group of the outlaws holed up on the eastern side of the house, and he did not doubt that the straw would be as dry as tinder, would burn like a torch.

'You're right,' he whispered. 'It's our only chance. Warn the rest of the men to be ready to move in once I give the signal.'

He slithered away through the bushes, long thorny strands cutting his face and hands, but he scarcely noticed them. Keeping his head as low as possible to avoid being seen from below, he reached the wagon a few moments later. Two blocks of wood had been set below the first pair of wheels to act as a brake and prevent it from rolling down the hill.

He climbed slowly to his feet, using the bulk of the wagon as a shield so that he could not be seen by any of the outlaws around the ranch.

Dimly, in the distance, he heard a harsh voice yell:

'This is your last chance, Ventner. I ain't going to warn you any more. Either throw out your guns and come on out, or we're coming in to get you. I've made you a fair offer. You get out of here, take your daughter with you, and we'll let you go free. You've got twenty seconds to make up your mind.'

'You don't fool me, Carson,' Ventner's voice roared back defiantly from the house. 'I've met up with your sort before. You'd shoot us down in cold blood the minute we stepped outside. I reckon that you and your hired killers want to rule this territory by fear. Well, you don't scare me none.'

That's the way to talk, thought Mark inwardly. *Don't let them get you down.*

'That your last word on the subject, Ventner?'

'Yeah, it is.' Ventner's words were still defiant. 'And the first of your killers to show himself will get his belly full of lead.'

Bart Carson yelled something in a bull-like voice. Instantly a fusillade of shots rang out around the whole perimeter of the house. The barn was still burning furiously, but fortunately the wind was not carrying the flames all the way across the intervening space to the house. If it did, the dry wood of the building would catch immediately and there was no doubt what would happen to the folk inside.

Mark waited no longer. A swift glance to either side told him that his men were now in position. The brief flare of the sulphur match would not have been visible from below, he felt sure of that. Holding the flaring match against the straw, it caught instantly. Dried out by long weeks in the hot sunlight, it flared up swiftly and savagely. It would be seen within seconds now, and he risked exposing himself to fire from down below, moving round to the sides and knocking the pieces of wood away from under the wheels. A swift push that wrenched the muscles of his shoulders sent the wagon moving off down the slope. Imperceptibly at first, then slowly and finally swiftly, it rolled downhill, straight for where the outlaws were all crouched low, firing into the ranch. It was a measure of their concentration on what they were doing that they did not see it until it was on their heels. Then it was to late for many of them.

The shrieks and yells were clearly audible above the outburst of gunfire as Kennedy and the other men opened up, shooting directly into the running, struggling men around the ranch. The blazing wagon gave off hardly any smoke. The straw burned only with flame, spilling burning straw over the men as it thundered through them, scattering them to every side.

In the red glare Mark saw one man rise up directly in front of the running wagon, throw up his arms, his mouth opening in shrieking fear, but any screams he may have uttered were lost completely, drowned as he fell back, the shafts of the wagon striking him full in the chest, hurling him like a puppet against the wall of the ranch, pinning him there.

Mark closed his eyes for an instant, feeling a rising nausea in the pit of his stomach. But it passed immediately. These men deserved all they got.

Taking his life in his hands, Mark went running down the slope, Colts blazing from the hip as he ran. Behind him the other ranchers were shooting with the Winchesters, picking off those of the outlaws who were still on their feet, still alive, trying to get away, to run for their horses, coming under fire from the hill and the house. Several of them fell long before they managed to reach their mounts. Bart Carson was yelling orders harshly at the top of his voice.

Mark reached the bottom of the slope, skirted the edge of the corral, ran forward, both guns blazing an arc of death as he advanced. He dropped three men before they could reach the horses. A fourth, picked off by Kennedy, dropped limply out of the saddle, his foot trailing in one stirrup. The horse reared at the sudden bedlam of noise, then started to run, dragging the man in the dust.

Mark barely gave him a second glance. Now that he and the others were closing in on the house, the shooting from the ranch had stopped, clearly recognising who they were. A bullet struck the hard ground close to his leg and chirruped away into the distance. Then the outlaws were riding out, firing as they went.

Evidently the men with Carson were totally demoralised, refused to listen to the orders he yelled, orders telling them to stand their ground and shoot it out, that they still outnumbered the defenders, even with these new arrivals. Mark ran for the porch; the door opened before he got there and Cal Ventner pushed his way out, the Colts still gripped in his hands.

Mark steadied him as he stumbled forward, eyes casting about for the gang that had besieged them during the night.

'Steady, Cal,' he said loudly. 'They're gone. I doubt if they'll be back. They've been beaten.' He didn't say that Bart Carson and possibly his brothers were still alive and that his revenge had gone unsated. He urged the other back into the house. 'Any casualties in here?'

Virginia Ventner came forward. She laid her Winchester against the wall in the corner of the room. Her voice sounded tired, but very steady.

'I think one of the other men was hit in the back room,

133

but I'm not sure. I'll go take a look.'

'Better make some coffee, too, Virginia,' said Cal, quietly. 'I reckon we need some.'

Dawn brightened in the east and threw a pale light over the ranch. The fire which had almost totally destroyed the barn had virtually burnt itself out.

Now that the excitement was over for the time being, the weariness was back in Mark's body, a deep-seated thing that he could not shake off. Yet he knew that he could not sleep, that the hate in his soul, twisting like a knife in the bowels, would not let him rest.

He went outside, into the cool early morning air, Kennedy and the other boys had removed the bodies which had littered the courtyard and corral. Most of them were unknown to Mark, but there were two which he recognised instantly. Brad and Matt Carson, two of the men who had been responsible for killing his sister all those years before. He had stood and stared down at their dead faces and a little of the tautness and the bitterness had drained out of him – but not all.

Bart Carson was still alive, had ridden away with the rest of the men. Until he was dead, Mark knew he would never be satisfied, would not sleep easy at nights.

The door of the ranch opened and he heard the light step behind him, a moment before Virginia Ventner said: 'I though I might find you here, Mark. You know, then, about two of the Carson brothers.'

He nodded.

'Brad and Matt? Sure, they're both dead.' He stared up at the sun, lying low on the skyline.

'You're a strange man, Mark Farrell,' said the girl, softly. Her hand lay on his arm as it had that night they had ridden back to the ranch, after they had narrowly escaped death at the hands of the Carsons and their band of hired killers. She smiled at him. It was a thin smile but told clearly of her amazement that he could still find bitterness in his heart.

'I wonder what it is that's kept you alive all this time, nursing that hatred deep inside you. Somehow, I don't think it was just the hate that's watched over you, bringing you to this moment.'

'You reckon that he might have decided to ride back into town? Maybe he figured that Sheriff Colman betrayed him, and he's gone there to settle the score.'

'You're still thinking about Bart Carson?' She looked up at him, studying his face closely, searching it as if trying to find there the answer to some of the questions that had been worrying her ever since she had known this man.

'I'll never stop thinking about him until I know he's dead or I've killed him myself.'

'And if he kills you? Why go out looking for trouble, why take the chance that you might be the one to die? Haven't you done enough, destroying those other two, breaking up that gang of killers that threatened the peaceful existence of the place?'

'Not until he's dead and I've paid my debt and kept my vow.'

There was a quality of stubbornness in his voice that Virginia Ventner recognised instantly, and knew that, no matter what she did or said, she could not fight. The hatred that was burned into this man as if by some branding iron could never be removed until he had finished what he had set out to do and neither she, nor anyone else, would be able to stop him.

'Maybe he has ridden into town,' she said finally. 'It's the only place there is for him to go, unless he decides to run for the border. He must know that you'll be coming for him. He'll be waiting for you if he is in town.'

'I realise that.'

He hitched his gunbelt higher, thumbed the hammers of the guns almost absently, but there was nothing absent about the tight look on his face or the flames that showed briefly at the back of his grey eyes.

'Very well, then. I won't stop you from riding out.' She took her hand away from his arm and stepped back a couple of paces. 'It seems that you're still determined to get yourself killed. If that's what you want, then I want no part of it.'

She turned quickly, not before he had seen the tears on her cheeks, and ran back on to the porch and into the house, slamming the door behind her.

The sun lifted from the horizon and brought the warmth with it. The few clouds that had come with the dawn faded swiftly. Out in the meadows the men were already at work, salvaging what they could from the barn, out rounding up the stray horses that had been stampeded from the corral. Soon, thought Mark, watching them at work, everything would be back to normal here on the ranch. Bart Carson had made his play and failed. But he was still alive, still around some place, and the mere thought of it tightened Mark's body, and he knew another moment of hard bitterness.

The wave of sunlight that had broken over the hills in the distance, shattering the night to pieces, touched the bushes and pines on the edge of the ranch with dark green shadow. He stood watching it for a long moment, engrossed in his own thoughts, scarcely aware now of the work that went on around him.

Then he turned and went over to the bunkhouse. Old Teeler stood in the doorway and watched him as he approached. There was a half amused look on his leathery features.

'Heard that you said, Mark, to Miss Virginia. You riding into town today to get Bart Carson?'

'That's right, old-timer.'

'Reckon you'd better keep a sharp eye on any windows overlooking the street if you do meet up with him. He's as crafty as a coyote. He'll have a *hombre* there with a Winchester behind one of those windows and if Bart don't drop you in the street, you can bet anything this other killer will.'

'Thanks for the warning.' Mark nodded tersely. 'I'll keep my eyes open.'

He went inside, ate breakfast slowly, aware of the looks of the other men in the long room, watching him covertly, trying to guess at the thoughts that ran through his mind at that moment. His face betrayed nothing.

Finishing his coffee, he pushed back his chair and got to his feet, checked the Colts in their holsters, dropping them back into the leather pouches.

The men continued to watch him closely as he turned on his heel and walked for the door. In the doorway he paused, looked back at the men gathered around the long wooden table.

'It could be that you'll be needing a new sheriff in Mason Bend later today,' he said soberly. 'And with Bart Carson out of the way, you might manage to elect your-selves an honest man to the job.'

Outside he picked up his horse from the corral, climbed up into the saddle. The night weariness was still on him, and he realised that it had been more than three days since he had had a proper night's rest. He flexed his fingers for a moment on the reins, then turned to ride out of the courtyard, but at that moment the door of the ranch house opened and Cal's voice called loudly to him.

Reining, he faced the other as the older man walked stiffly across the courtyard. He came right up to where Mark sat in the saddle, held the bridle with his right hand, looking up at the other's face.

'I reckon you know what you're doing, Mark,' he said soberly. 'When a man has to do something like this, when he has to work bitterness and hatred out of his system, then there's nothing anyone else can do to stop him. But

I want you to know that I've been watching you carefully ever since you rode in here and asked for that job. I've changed my mind about a lot of things as far as you're concerned.'

He paused, glanced down at the ground under his feet for a moment, then looked back. There was a curious expression on his face, one that Mark had never seen before.

'I suppose it's only natural that when a man has managed to build something as big as this ranch out of nothing, built it with his bare hands from some of the worst country in the state, fought to keep it, he would have liked a son to pass it on to. I don't have a son, Mark, I have only my daughter Virginia, and I know, myself, how she feels about you. Before you go, I want you to know that I'd be glad to have you marry her, to take over this place when I die.'

Mark sat looking at him for a long moment, not knowing what to say. There seemed to be no answer to that, or if there were, what was it?

'I'm only sorry that I have to do this, Cal,' he said softly, finally.

As the other man stepped back, a faint smile on his face, he heard Ventner say: 'I reckon I would have thought the less of you if you didn't go, Mark.'

But he could not be sure as he rode out of the courtyard, taking the trail into the hills, setting his face towards the red glow of the rising sun.

Hours later he checked his mount on a rise of ground that looked out over the broad lands leading down into the deep river valley. A tired man who had ridden hard and fast all the way from the ranch, now many miles behind him. Grey-eyed, black-browed, with an iron will and a grim, murderous determination that nothing could shake, a bitter hatred that drove him on when all else failed.

Mason Bend lay ahead now, only a few short miles away. Close now, close enough that another few hours' ride would bring him face to face with Bart Carson, the man he had sworn to kill.

Below, and a mile or so distant, the river was a twisting course of silver in the afternoon sun, the heat head still building up over the scene. Sitting there, he ran a dry tongue over his lips, then turned his head slowly, keen eyes quartering the horizon. The plain that stretched below him lay deserted. Not a single cloud of dust thrown up by a rider spotted the surface.

The contours of the land, the direction taken by the river itself, told him that, although he had ridden across strange country to reach this spot, coming out of the hills on to the plains at an unfamiliar point and from an unfamiliar direction, he knew almost exactly where he was. The silence about him on that hot, yellow, sunblazed afternoon was so still that he felt he had just to reach out a hand to touch it. A deep and strangely tangible thing which crowded around him, unmoving.

Gigging his mount, he rode down into the long valley, the sun glare beating dully against his brain, even through closed lids. High up over his head the buzzards wheeled in slow, endless circles like tattered strips of black cloth, sailing lazily against the harsh, blue-white mirror of the heavens.

On the bank of the river he dismounted, filled his canteen, drank deep of the cool, clear water, then refilled the canteen to the brim, pushing in the cork. Pushing back his hat on to his head, he squatted there among the hot, smooth rocks that edged the water, letting his mount drink.

He rested there for a while, getting his thoughts into some sort of order in his mind. Two of the Carsons were dead, shot down outside the Ventner ranch house, killed probably because they had never paused to consider the possibility of defeat, the chance that the tables might be turned against them. Only the one left now of the original three.

The man who had, according to the testimony of the injured passenger in that stage, been the one who pulled the trigger that had shot his sister.

For a second the angry bitterness flooded everything else out of his mind, blurring his vision as he knelt there, and his fingers flexed and unflexed on his knees as if they were curled around the triggers of his own guns and he already had Bart Carson in his sights.

He stepped up into the stirrup, swung into the saddle. The utter weariness in his body was something he seemed to have been forced to live with for almost as long as he could remember. An ache that dwelt in every single muscle and fibre of his being. His eyelids were lined with dust and grit, eyes burning every time he blinked.

Fording the wide, shallow stretch of the river, he put the sun at his back, turned east and rode slowly now, between the rising buttes, towards Mason Bend, letting the sorrel have its head.

Night reached in from the east, his shadow lengthened and fled before him, and still Mark Farrell had not reached town. He had taken his time during the long hours of the afternoon and evening, knowing that if Carson had headed back to Mason Bend he would still be there.

The odds were that there was no other place for him to go, that he knew he could not run far enough or fast enough to escape the man who hunted him down. Like a cornered rat, now was the time when he had to turn and fight.

And only in this town, with Sheriff Colman in his pay, could he consider himself to be safe from the law. This was where he would make his stand.

He pushed his gaze ahead of him as he rode into the

approaching darkness. The air was clear and cool here after the harsh, dry pressure of the plains, and he breathed deeply of it, glad of the brief chance to relax for a little while.

By lifting his head a little, he could make out the faint yellow lights of the town in the distance, but there seemed to be a faint mist over the trail that lay in that direction. He felt a trifle more assured inwardly now that he had got this far without trouble.

At the back of his mind, nagging him continually during the long afternoon, had been the thought that maybe not all of Carson's men had deserted him after the gun battle back at the ranch, that some had stuck by him, and they would lay an ambush for him – for Carson would know that very soon he would be on his trail.

The mere fact that there had been no trouble so far along the trail was reassuring. It meant that it was now more than likely that Bart Carson was alone in Mason Bend – an isolated man just as he was himself.

He stretched himself up carefully in the saddle, peering ahead, eyes probing the shadows, keeping a tight grip on the reins.

Whatever else he might be, Bart Carson was not a coward. He was reputed to be a very fast man with a gun, had been known to have killed several men down on the borders, although whether in fair fight nobody seemed to know; and now that the showdown had come, Mark doubted if he would turn tail and run.

He had the inescapable feeling that they would meet again in Mason Bend, meet face to face, with guns in their hands, and he knew with certainty that only one of them would walk away from that encounter.

Behind him the sun vanished in a flash of flame that was like a distant explosion on the rim of the world, so that he half-expected to hear the sound of it going down. Sitting easy in the saddle, he thought back over what Cal

Ventner had said to him just before he had ridden out, turning the words over in his mind. Was it possible that with Bart Carson dead, with all of the bitterness and anger washed clear of his mind, he could find peace back there with Virginia?

He would have liked to think so, would have liked to feel that he could forget the fighting, the long, lonely days and nights on the prairie, camped out under the stars with only the ground for his bed and a hat for a pillow. He tried to recall what it had been like in the old days, before his sister had been killed, before the war had come even, and turned men into something worse than beasts.

But no matter how he tried, everything seemed dim and misty, and he could remember nothing. After a while, approaching the outskirts of Mason Bend, he pushed even that out of his mind and forced himself to concentrate only on the one thing uppermost in his mind.

He had circled the town, so that he came in from the east. If Carson were watching the street, he would be expecting him to ride in from the other end of town. For a moment he paused, reining his horse at the very end of the street, casting his gaze along it, eyeing the shafts of yellow light that spilled out of the windows of the saloons and stores.

The sound of a tinny piano came from the nearest saloon, and there was the discordant sound of men singing at the tops of their voices.

The place looked and seemed peaceful enough on the face of it. But he had seen too many towns like this during his long career and he knew never to take things on trust, never to trust the surface appearance.

In the darkness he knew that he had not been seen, and he gigged the sorrel forward, very slowly, making scarcely any sound, keeping in to the shadows as much as possible.

A quarter of the way along the main street he reined the horse, slipped from the saddle, and tied the bridle to one of the hitching poles.

For a moment he debated whether to take the Winchester with him, then decided against it. He had always preferred to use the slim-handled Colts whenever he met men face to face.

The street in front of him, stretching away like a river of midnight, except where the light fell on the dry, dusty surface, was strangely quiet. Had the townsfolk seen Bart Carson ride into town and knew what it had meant, knew that there was trouble a-brewing, and that soon, close on his heels, another man would come riding in, a man nursing a grievance, itching to kill?

Horses stood patiently and quietly along the wooden rails at the sides and, here and there, in the shadows, further along, he caught the glowing tips of cigarettes winking in the darkness, and knew that there were men there, taking it easy in the cool of the night, smoking silently along the boardwalks. But the street itself was dark and empty.

His gaze flickered over to the sheriff's office. There was no light inside, and it came to him that perhaps the other had already taken the advice he had given him and had left town, riding out somewhere, where he figured he might be safe from the law. For the past few years he had made a mockery of law and order. Now it would be hot on his tail.

His eyes were cold and his jaw set as he made his way softly and swiftly across the street, hugging the dark shadows on the other side, slipping in the direction of the sheriff's office. There was just the chance that the other might not yet have left town, and if that were so, he might conceivably know where Carson was hiding out. If he did, it might make things a lot easier for him.

Grimly he hitched up the wide gunbelt, narrowed his eyes as he reached the intersection of the streets, and glanced swiftly about him. Nobody seemed to have noticed him.

Like a shadow, equally as silent, he edged past the front of the hotel, angled over the road and a few moments later was holed up in the shadows at the side of the jailhouse.

Carefully he checked everything, then moved around to the rear, determined to take no chances. The sheriff still wanted to see him dead for the humiliation he had caused him, and he would be just as tricky about it as Carson was likely to be.

The door at the rear of the building was open. Cautiously he opened it and slipped inside, into pitch blackness. He dared not strike a match, and moved forward by sense of feel alone, relying on his memory of the place when he had been locked up there. Moments later he felt the hard, cold steel of the bars of the cells, knew exactly where he was.

The place seemed as empty and silent as a tomb. Nothing seemed to move, and he could hear the sound of his own heart thumping slowly and steadily against his ribs, and the faint whisper of his jacket against the smooth walls of the passage.

Somewhere ahead of him would be the door which led through into the sheriff's office. If Colman was still in town, that was where he would be. Maybe getting ready to leave, but determined that he was not going to go empty-handed.

Slowly he edged forward, one of the Colts whispering into his right hand. He reached the door, found that it was lying half open, and pushed it with the flat of his left hand, narrowing his eyes.

The office was in total darkness.

Cautiously he made his way forward, scarcely able to see. He caught his shin on the side of the desk, froze for a long moment, his finger extending the pressure on the trigger of the gun in his hand in involuntary action. If there was anyone in the room standing in the shadows, waiting to shoot him down before he was even aware of their presence, this was when the bullet would come. But there was no other sound in the room.

He let his breath out in a long sigh. Evidently the sheriff had decided to quit while he had the chance. Possibly by now he would be miles away from Mason Bend, thought Mark, and they would never see him again in that territory.

At least the town had not lost by the other's action. But it meant that he would be unable to find anyone who might talk with a gun in their ribs and tell him just where Bart Carson was.

Slowly, not wanting to be heard by anyone outside, he edged around the desk, moving in the direction of the door. Another step and he half fell over something soft and yielding.

Clutching at the desk for a moment, he stared down at the floor, then went down on one knee, pouching the gun in its holster.

There was no doubt that the man who lay behind the desk was dead. There was the stickiness of blood between his shoulder blades where he had been shot in the back. He risked being seen, striking a sulphur match and letting the brief red glare rest on the dark features that stared up at him from the floor. As he had suspected, it was Sheriff Colman.

The match died out between his fingers and he rose slowly to his feet. It began to add up. Bart Carson had possibly figured that the sheriff had been the man who had betrayed him. He would have known that Mark had come riding into town with a handful of men and that he had stopped off to have a little talk with Colman. He had come back himself to settle the score.

Going over to the window, he stood there, keeping well back into the room, staring out into the street, trying to formulate a plan.

He knew, as yet, nothing of what Carson meant to do; knew nothing of how many men he had with him. It would be both foolish and suicidal to try to fight his way in to the other through a ring of hired guns. There was too great an element of risk attached to that. So far his luck had held but, sooner or later, if he persisted in pushing it, it would give out on him. The knowledge lay heavy and solid on his mind.

Leaving the sheriff's body where it lay, he went back along the passage and out through the rear entrance. There came the sound of shooting from one of the saloons, but he paid no heed to it. Merely some of the men letting off steam, it signified nothing.

Working his way around the side of the building, he entered the main street and walked openly towards the nearest saloon.

He had already made up his mind what he had to do; face Carson openly, give him fair warning. The sight of the sheriff lying back there with that bullet hole in his back had somehow changed his mind for him. He did not want to have to live with his conscience, knowing that he had hunted down a man and shot him in the back without giving fair warning.

Reaching the saloon, he pushed open the doors and stepped inside. Almost at once the noise ceased, as if someone had dropped a blanket over everything. He stood quite still for a moment, letting his gaze wander around the saloon, from the men standing at the bar to the others round the tables.

When he was finally satisfied that Carson was not there, he walked over to the bar, stared at the bartender.

'Whiskey,' he said quietly.

This was the saloon where Clem Hagberg had tried to gun him down – and failed. The large mirror at the back of the bar showed everyone clearly to his questing gaze. No one moved as the bartender, his face a curious pasty shade, brought the bottle and glass and poured out a slug for him, then stepped back along the polished bar. He kept wary eyes on Mark.

'Tell that *hombre* to go on playing.'

Without lifting his head, Mark spoke to the other, saw the man start, then turn and signal something to the man behind the piano. The other hesitated, then started up a tinkling melody and, after a momentary pause, the gamblers went back to their games and the men returned to their places at the bar.

'Looking for anybody in particular?' The man standing next to Mark glanced round at him.

'Perhaps.'

'Wouldn't be Bart Carson, would it?' There was a strangely covert amusement on the others features.

'It might be. Know where I could find him?'

'He's in town some place.' The other seemed mighty anxious to talk. 'I saw him come riding back just before midday. Seems in one hell of a hurry. Had a handful of men with him, but they rode out before nightfall.'

'Know why they left him?'

'Heard there was some mighty hard words spoken in the saloon along the street. The others reckoned that they weren't going to ride with him any longer, and said something about him being the only one left, and if he had any sense he'd hightail it outa town while he had the chance.'

'But he's still here.' In spite of himself, there was a harsh note in Mark's voice. 'You're sure of that?'

The other had a sly humour on his face, shifty, beady eyes. But there was a kind of wisdom in his gaze as if he knew a lot more than he was telling.

'You're Mark Farrell. Thought I knew you. I reckon you'll be the one who's riding in after Carson.'

'That's right. Now suppose that you tell me where he is.'

The other shook his head.

'Reckon you might as well make yourself comfortable, mister. Carson won't come out to face you until he's good and ready. He's holed up somewhere, but he'll stay out of sight until he's ready to meet you.'

'How do you know all this?' demanded Mark harshly.

'I know Carson. That's his way. I've seen him meet more than a dozen men, and always it's the same. He's killed them all at sun-up.'

Mark nodded, sipped the whiskey in his glass, drained it, then poured himself another drink. It wasn't quite what he had expected. But the old ways of violence, of sudden death, were never changing, never different. They would work their way through this little town, through the small period of time without any variation. It might have been a trap, but somehow he doubted it.

Picking up the bottle, he took it with him to one of the tables, lowered himself into the chair and sat alone, drinking slowly.

Around him men came and went as the night passed slowly, the hours ticking away. The gamblers at the various tables flicked out their cards or dice, men won or lost their money or gold dust, and the bare-shouldered girls at the far end of the saloon took coin in their own way.

Mark watched it all but it seemed to have no meaning for him. He had seen similar scenes in towns all over the west. They never seemed to change, and often he wondered if this country was ever going to grow up, to shake the dust of its beginning off its feet and start to grow, to expand, to bring in the merchants and bankers, to settle down as it would have to do before long. Then, when that day came, there would be no place for the bandits, the killers and the two-bit gamblers. They would have passed into history along with so many other things.

The saloons in Mason Bend never closed, and the man seated alone at the table, with the whiskey bottle in front of him, staring straight before him, a man with a hard face and grey eyes, never slept. There was the power of hatred in him, and that transcended everything else, drove out the want for sleep, the need for rest.

Outside the night passed slowly, the sky still dark, the moon moving to its last quarter, lighting the street. Everything seemed quiet now. Once Mark heard a horse move along the street, out of town, but he paid it no heed.

A little before four o'clock in the morning, while it was still dark, the old man who had spoken to him earlier that evening pushed open the swing doors, came in, and walked over to his table.

'I've just seen Carson,' he said in a thin voice. 'He sent a message for me to give to you.'

'Go on,' said Mark tightly.

'He'll meet you in town at sun-up. Unless you want to ride out now and keep on riding.'

'I'll be here.'

Mark tilted the bottle, poured the last dregs of whiskey into the glass, and downed it in a single gulp.

'I'll tell him that.'

The other backed away, threw a swift glance in the direction of the man behind the bar, then vanished out into the street. The doors swung together for an instant, then stilled.

Dawn was still a far-off thing in the sky, a faint glistening of grey, when Mark Farrell stirred at the table. He had not slept that night, but had sat there, with only the bartender watching him with a puzzled expression on his face.

A little while later a negro came in and began to brush the place out with a twig broom, sweeping the dirt and litter out through the batwing doors and on to the street.

The bartender came over and stood beside the table looking down at him.

'You want that I should fix you something to eat?' he asked. 'Bacon and eggs and some black coffee maybe.'

Mark shook his head.

'Keep it until I get back,' he said harshly, getting stiffly to his feet. He walked over to the windows and stared out, looking along the street. It was still dark. The sun would not be up for another half-hour, and he knew that he had been foolish to refuse the offer of breakfast.

He tightened his lips, ran his tongue around his mouth. Somewhere out there Bart Carson would be waiting, he told himself fiercely. Soon one of them would be lying dead in the dust of the main street.

Absently he eased the Colts in their holsters, then let them drop back into place. This was the moment he had waited for and dreamed of all these years. Something he had often never expected to happen. It was still incredible that Carson should have stayed in town to face him, instead of riding out once his men deserted him, and he knew that everything was lost. The only explanation for the other's behaviour that Mark could think of was that Carson held a similar hatred for him.

He had been the one who had really upset all of the outlaw's plans for domination of this part of the state. Had he not arrived on the scene and thrown in his lot with Ventner, it might have been comparatively easy for the other and his brothers to take over the entire area, which included some of the richest grazing ground in the whole of Kansas.

And they had made sure of getting the law on their side from the very beginning. It had been fortunate for them that the town had had a crooked sheriff, and they had been able to control him.

Maybe, though, they had known that long before they had come here to Mason Bend. Maybe it had all been part of their plan before they had busted out of jail.

He let the thoughts run through his mind, following them to their logical conclusion. That had to be it. Somehow, those three outlaws had known about Colman being sheriff. Maybe he had even engineered their break-out from jail in Dodge.

Once here, they would be safe from the law. Even if the United States marshals or the Rangers decided to come snooping around, they would come up against a blank wall as far as the sheriff was concerned. And once they had the Ventner ranch, that would be the end of law and order as far as the decent ordinary citizens of Mason Bend were concerned.

He clenched his hands into tight-balled fists by his sides. There was a lot to settle with this man Carson, he thought tightly. He wondered if the people of the town would ever realise just how much.

Out of the corner of his eye he saw the old man coming back along the street, keeping well into the middle. Evidently the other intended taking no chances on getting shot.

Inwardly, watching him, Mark wondered where the other citizens of the town had gone, whether they had been warned of the violence which was likely to break out very soon.

Certainly it looked to be an uneasy kind of town. It had that curious waiting quality hanging over it which Mark had sensed on several previous occasions.

The doors swung open. The old man came in, grinned foolishly. He walked over to Mark.

'You still here?' he said harshly. 'I figured you might have ridden out before now.'

'Now you know different,' said Mark thinly. 'You been to see Carson again?'

'Nope. Don't know where he is. Around some place, I guess. He'll come out shooting when he's good and ready.'

'That's just fine.' Mark spoke coldly. He said softly: 'I suppose you know about Colman?'

'The sheriff?' The other shook his greying head. 'What's happened?' He paused, eyed Mark warily. 'Come to think of it, I ain't seen the sheriff around since noon yesterday.'

'You won't find him around any longer,' muttered Mark grimly. 'He's dead. You'll find him lying on the floor behind the desk in his office. He's been shot in the back. I reckon if you want to know who did it, you'll find the answer pretty soon.'

'Carson,' guessed the other shrewdly.

He stared out of the window to where the dawn was brightening slowly, dimming the stars. The moon had dropped to the western horizon and it too was paling before the light of the coming day.

'That's right. He was using Colman for his own ends. He had to have the law on his side until he was big enough to dispense with him, so he bought Colman as soon as he rode into town. Colman was scared of these men, anyway.'

'Then why did he kill the sheriff? Surely he needed every man he could get?'

'He had to have men with him that he could trust. He wouldn't want anyone riding behind him who might try to shoot him in the back if things went wrong. And they did go wrong. Both of his brothers have been killed and most of the men he took with him when he tried to take the Ventner place. He's finished and he reckons that Colman betrayed him, warned us where he was headed, and enabled us to get back to the ranch in time to turn the tables on him.'

The other gave him a studying glance and, for a moment, some other question seemed to be balanced in his mind. Then he clamped his lips tightly together and shrugged his lean, stooping shoulders, making a small motion with his hand.

'Why tell me all this?' he asked after a pause. 'Could it be because you ain't sure which of you is going to come out of this duel alive and you want me to know so I can tell the others?'

Mark watched the other's lips change and form a new, speculative shape, and his bright eyes never left the younger man's face.

'Think what you like,' he said tersely, 'but I just thought you might like to know.'

It seemed a long time before Mark pushed the doors of the saloon open and stepped down into the dust of the street. On either side of him the street stretched away to the very edge of town, empty, utterly deserted. There was no one on the boardwalks and only one horse was in sight, his own, tethered where he had left it, perhaps fifty yards away.

The only sign of life was the old man, who stood just inside the doorway of the saloon, watching him with the same expression he had noted before when he had first met the other, direct and speculative, barely showing interest.

Turning on his heel, he moved very slowly along the street, keeping well in to the middle. There was no telling where Carson might be at that moment, perhaps even watching him from some place of concealment, waiting the right moment to leap out into the open and go for his guns.

He recalled what Cal Ventner had told him of the man. The way he might have another killer perched behind one of the windows overlooking the street, a rifle aimed at his heart.

Acting on instinct, he lifted his gaze, ran it along the upper storeys of the buildings on either side of the street. There was nothing there to make him suspicious.

He walked on, his feet making barely any sound in the soft dust. The silence which lay over everything merely served to heighten the tension in his body and mind. The boardwalks were too damned full of shadows for his liking and, at any moment, he expected to hear a sudden yell, a harsh shout, followed by the slamming blast of a Colt and the shattering impact of the leaden slug as it ploughed through his body. But the silence continued and seemed to grow more intense.

He paused half way along the street, looked about him. He saw the faces at the windows of the houses near by, saw them being pulled back as if their owners were afraid to let themselves be seen.

Everyone had got off the streets, he thought tightly. So everyone knew that violence was about to break loose. He rubbed the haze of weariness from his eyes and drew in a deep breath of the cool morning air that flowed along the street.

The dust had not yet risen, had not yet been kicked up by the hoofs of horses riding through.

He ran a dry tongue over equally dry lips, began to wish that he had not drank that whiskey during the night. It might have been better, he reasoned, if he had gone out and hunted Carson down like the animal he was. At least, it would have been over by now – one way or the other.

Tension crackled along the street of Mason Bend. Still no sign of Carson.

For a moment Mark had the feeling that perhaps the other had really slipped away during the night, that the show of waiting for sun-up had been nothing more than a ruse to keep him here in the saloon while the other made good his getaway. By now he could be miles away, heading for the border. Down in New Mexico there were a thousand places where an outlaw like Carson might hide, where it would be impossible to locate him. The thought almost broke him in half.

But he walked on, eyes flicking swiftly from side to side, seeking the man he had come all this way to kill. Behind him the grey of the dawn was slowly changing to the blood red of sun-up. Already it was touching the crests of the mountains on the skyline. Soon it would be in the streets of Mason Bend.

Ahead of Mark there was only a short, empty stretch of

the street leading out of town. He knew that Carson would not be there.

Very slowly he paused, then turned and started back, and it was at that moment, just as he was ready to move back, retracing his steps towards the middle of the town, that the tall, stocky figure stepped out from the boardwalk, stood with feet braced apart in the middle of the street, more than a hundred yards away.

Bart Carson!

Mark felt the blood suddenly begin to pulse redly along his veins. His eyes were narrowed to mere slits now, and he knew why the other had allowed him to go past, forcing him to turn and face him in that direction. Now he had the rays of the rising sun full in his eyes, making it more difficult to see the figure that stood for an instant in the distance and then began to walk very slowly in his direction, hands held a few short inches above the butts of the Colts in their holsters.

There was a long moment of utter silence. Carson had cleverly seen to it that he had the advantage. It told Mark that the other was taking no chances, and his gaze flickered for the barest fraction of a second above the advancing figure, searching swiftly and intently along the buildings on either side.

Was there the slightest flicker of movement at the back of any of these windows, the faintest glimmer of red sunlight winking on the barrel of a Winchester that might at that very moment be pointing in his direction, lining up on his chest, ready to spit death at any sudden signal from the bull-necked man, who came forward very slowly?

He could see nothing, but he was not satisfied. He did not believe that the other really meant to face him on equal terms. There was some trick here and he had to discover what it was before it was too late. Carson would want everyone in town to see that he had outdrawn this man who had hunted him down, but he was not such a fool as to believe that he could outdraw the man who faced him, less than seventy yards away. He would not take that risk, anyway.

So he had someone else hidden away somewhere, drawing a bead on him that very instant. Mark felt a tiny shiver pass along his spine. His eyes flickered in every direction, seeking trouble, but not finding any.

Carson paused when he was less than forty yards away. There was a faint sneer written all over his fleshy, heavily jowled features. Loudly, he called:

'I hear you've been looking for me, Farrell. Well, you've found me.'

'That's right, Carson.'

Anger thinned Mark's voice, but he held himself under rigid control. He had the impression that the other was deliberately trying to taunt him, endeavouring to make him careless.

'What's your quarrel with me, Farrell?'

'You know well enough. That stage you held up outside Dodge before they arrested you, the woman you shot down, just for fun, that was my sister. I swore then that some day I'd meet up with you and kill you.'

The other threw back his head and laughed loudly.

'I've heard of you, Farrell. They say that you're a fast man with a gun. Maybe you are, but this is where you've met your match.'

Out of the corner of his eye, Mark saw some of the men from the town gathered at the ends of the street. They would take no part in the shooting, he knew that, they were there to see what happened. But somewhere close by there was another man, waiting to kill him. Carson sounded too cocky and assured.

With an effort he let his gaze move away from the man in front of him, knowing the risk he took. Carson could see every expression on his face, would take advantage of any unguarded moment. His hands were just above his guns, ready to drop and fire.

Every house seemed deserted. Could it be that Carson had been too clever for him, that the assassin was behind him at this very moment at his back, there ready to fire?

The thought dwelt within him for a moment and was then rejected. Carson would not be such a fool as to have him shot in the back. He narrowed his gaze still further, unfocusing it.

It was then that he caught the sudden movement at the very edge of his vision. It had been so slight that it might have passed entirely unnoticed had he not been ready for it. He fixed his attention on it for an instant, then relaxed, facing Carson once again. He was completely on balance once more.

From the other's face he saw that the killer had seen this sudden change in him, and there was little doubt that he knew the reason. He knew that Mark had seen his accomplice and a look of fear flashed momentarily over his fleshy features.

Then, in a sudden blur of speed, his hands dropped, snaking for the guns in his belt. A fast draw – yet not so fast as that of the man who faced him. Down and up, Mark lifted the Colts in a smooth, sweeping draw that lifted the line of muzzles above the line of fire. A single snap of the wrists brought them into line with their targets and the pressure on the triggers followed a split second later.

Sound bucketed along the street, sharp, piecing echoes that rang from one side to the other. Mark's lips were flattened, drawn away from his teeth. Carson fired but was dropping forward even as he pressed the triggers with the last ounce of his failing strength. The bullets tore into the dust several feet in front of where Mark Farrell stood, straddle-legged.

Behind Carson, as he fell, several yards behind, there was the shattering of glass, a sudden yell blended with fear and pain, and a body toppled from one of the windows overlooking the street and crashed through the flimsy veranda on to the boardwalk. The rifle which had been clutched in the man's hand lay in the road some feet away from his body.

Mark's arms lowered. He pouched the guns wearily. For a moment he seemed unable to take anything in. He knew that there were men and women on the street now, coming out of the buildings or from the far ends of the town. But there was a vast eternity of unfeeling in his body.

Slowly he walked forward, one foot in front of the other, until he stood over the fallen body of Bart Carson, lying in the dust. There was blood on his chest, soaking into the shirt front, the stain widening, with blood on the dust of the road.

With an effort he stood erect, pulled a deep breath into his flaring nostrils. It was finished, he told himself fiercely. It was all over.

He had kept his vow and the man he had hunted for so many years now lay dead at his feet. He felt nothing against the other now. All of that, the hatred and the deep-seated bitterness, had been burned out of him, leaving him strangely empty inside. There seemed to be a void within him, and nothing new with which it could be filled.

The old man he had spoken to in the saloon came hurrying forward and stared wide-eyed at the man on the ground, then he looked up at Mark.

'Bart Carson dead,' he said, and his voice was little more than a hushed whisper. 'And his accomplice, as well.'

There seemed to be a lot of people talking at once, voices questioning and answering. Mark listened to them for a moment, then turned on his heel and walked to where his horse stood tethered at the hitching post. No one there made a move to stop him from leaving.

As he rode his body kept drooping forward in the saddle. The heat of the noon sun lay heavy on him and sweat ran into his eyes as he lowered his head over the saddle-horn. He seemed burned out. All of the fire was gone and had brought nothing to take its place. As the day passed he crossed the alkali flats, forded the river at the same point as he had on the previous day, and rode up through the stretches of timber, back in the direction of the Ventner ranch.

He scarcely noticed the sun as it continued its slow wheel of the heavens and began to fall down the western slope of the sky after touching its zenith. Not until the shadows began to fall and the coolness came with the freshening breeze that sprang up and blew down the sides of the hills, did he jerk up his head, look about him and take any interest in his surroundings.

His mount had made better time than he had imagined. Another five miles should see him at the ranch.

He drank deeply of the cool air, felt it go down into his tired lungs and bring new life into his body. His legs and arms ached and he stretched them in the stirrups, trying to relieve the incipient stabs of cramp which lanced through his limbs.

Quietly the horse traversed the rocks and entered the green of the pasturelands. Somehow he had the feeling that he was almost home; that after all of these long, weary years and miles, there was something more ahead for him than the endless wandering and the loneliness which had been his lot for so long.

The sun went down behind the western horizon, a jagged undulating horizon of tall peaks which seemed to hold the rosy hue of the setting sun long after the rest of the countryside was in deep shadow.

Night came to the valleys far earlier and more quickly than it did to the mountains. Then even that glow was gone and darkness covered everything. The stars were out in their thousands, a pale diffuse glow in the heavens.

Topping the low rise, he found himself staring down at

the ranch house. There were yellow lights showing warmly in the windows, and in the corral the horses had all been rounded up, while on the gentle slope directly in front of him the herd lowed softly as they milled around before settling down for the night.

He put his mount to the slope, kicked his spurs into its flanks for the first time since leaving Mason Bend.

He had just reached the courtyard when the door of the ranch house was flung open. Silhouetted against the yellow glow of the light behind her, he saw Virginia Ventner standing there, peering out uncertainly into the night.

Then she caught sight of him, ran forward with a glad little cry as he slid from the saddle.

At the sight of her all of his weariness seemed to vanish. He patted the horse's rump as he sent it into the corral, then turned as Virginia ran up to him, straight into his arms.

He saw her face lift a little, and he said: 'I had the feeling as I rode over the rise that I was really coming home this time. It's something I've never felt before, Virginia.'

Her smile was a warm thing in the shadows of her face. She didn't move away at the pressure of his arms.

'It took a lot of time and a lot of misery to find this,' he said quietly.

Slowly they made their way towards the house.